Nightstalker
Incorporated

Dedication

Dad. Enough said.

Acknowledgments

Diane, Dorene, Tammy and Tom
Without your invaluable contributions and encouragement, this book would have never happened.
Here's to the best team a guy could ask for
Thanks
Art

Like what you read? Questions? Comments? Let me know.

https://www.facebook.com/Art-DeForest-17030446 89948412/

http://www.amazon.com/-/e/B01CDKZA0O

1

"Pour it on!" I shouted, as the vampire came at us. It moved so fast you could barely see it. We had it isolated in a hallway, though, so each of my shooters took a section of the hall and poured fire into it. I was using the Saiga 12 gauge in my hand to try for aimed shots. Any monster can be brought down if you do enough damage fast enough. Sure the old tried and true methods worked. Staking, beheading, silver for werewolves, etc. We were prepared to go that route too if it came to it, but using handheld weapons against a monster was a surefire way to find yourself being treated like a human snack cake more often than not.

My team and I did everything in our power to never let that happen. Victory through superior firepower was our mantra, and we lived it daily.

The vamp jerked and stumbled repeatedly as it tried to reach us, screaming like a fallen death metal angel. The sheer volume of fire, caused it to lose its balance and move ever slower as the bones supporting his structure broke under a hail of double ought buckshot. It finally fell in a disjointed heap a couple feet from my shield wall. That's right, shield wall.

For every one of my guys or gals packing a Saiga, there was a teammate packing a kevlar riot shield. When some of the monsters could paralyze with a touch, keeping them off of you got really important.

Fire poured into the body for a couple more seconds as the vamp lay there twitching. "Hold fire!" I said finally over the team's comm. "Petey, finish him," I commanded. The shield wall broke apart as Petey stood up, and up, and up. He was a mountain. 6'9" of solid muscle and bone. He drew a hand axe from its spot on his pack as he stepped forward. The vamp was still keening and trying to get at us as Petey brought the wide curving blade of the double-bitted axe crashing down on the vamps neck. The sudden silence was almost shocking.

With a jerk, Petey pulled the axe from the carpeted floor now covered by vampire ash. The good thing about vampires was that it only took a vacuum to clean up the remains. The rest of the hallway, the adjoining offices, and most of the windows were going to take a little renovation to get them back to top shape once more. That was the problem with fully automatic 12 gauge shotguns. Not my problem, but a problem.

My problem was that someone had turned this formerly mild-mannered accounts manager into a ravening undead creature of the night and then left it to its own devices. I needed to have a chat with whoever had done that. It was probably going to be fatal.

Vampires weren't always the bad guys Hollywood made them out to be. They weren't often teen heartthrobs either. They damn sure didn't sparkle.

For the most, part they tended to be well to do business types who were more concerned with money, honor, and family. In that order. This tended to make most of them jerks in my opinion. They were jerks you could work with if you had to, though. Especially if some rogue was making babies and letting them run around feral. That was a serious no-no among the families. A new vamp was basically nothing but a ravening beast for at least the first year of its life. They were kept isolated as far from humans as possible until their mind came back and they learned some control.

We finished clearing the office building just to make sure there wasn't a second baby running around. If the pattern held, there wouldn't be, but better safe than sorry. This was the second vamp we'd been called out on in the last month.

We trooped out of the main entrance of the building, and I stopped at the police barricade where Lieutenant Alex Stevenson waited for us impatiently. The rest of my guys headed to the truck.

"Jesus Christ, Dale. What the hell were you fighting up there? I thought the whole building was going to collapse from all the lead you put into it."

I sighed tiredly. "Another baby. It took everything we had to stop it short of the shield wall." I said, shaking my head. "He was a fast little fucker. And don't take the lord's name in vain." I said as an afterthought.

Alex ran his hand through his hair in frustration. "Can't you guys keep it quieter? People thought you were starting WW3 or something."

"We don't work that way, and you know it," I said sternly. "We get the job done our way, period. Feel free not to use our services if you think you and your boys can do a better job."

Alex's face got hard as he stared me in the eye. "Dammit Dale, I don't deserve that bullshit." He seethed

It was my turn to look down and sigh. "I know....sorry," I said reluctantly.

Alex was a good guy, for a cop. He was our liaison with Chicago PD. That's right all you conspiracy theorists, the government knows about monsters and is hiding the fact from you. They will do almost anything to keep that secret too, so keep your trap shut or they'll shut it for you.

"Two babies in the same area in a week has me jumpy, I guess." I continued. "That means I have to go have a talk with Siobhan. You know how I love that." I said with a grimace.

Alex got a sloppy grin on his face. "I'm sure she'd love to make your get together much more pleasant." He said, making his eyebrows go up and down.

I snorted and gave him a shove in return. For some unknown reason, Siobhan O'Malley, the local master vampire for this area, had the hots for one Dale Frost. I'm not sure why. I'm just a guy. Sure I'm big and strong, but not near as big and strong as Petey. Yeah, I had a brain, but it didn't hold a candle to Smoke's. He was our gun and gadget guy.

The main problem was that down deep inside, where my inner caveman lived, I was tempted. Gorgeous was putting it mildly. Wavy auburn hair and emerald green eyes. You know the type. Creamy white skin and a body that made men and some women sin just to look at her. Yeah, she was to die for...literally I think. That's what kept me away from her. I had no interest in waking up dead one morning.

I promised I'd work on the noise issue and gave Alex a half wave as I headed for the truck that would take us back to headquarters.

++++

He crouched on the roof, hidden by the night and watching as the men in heavy black clothing walked from the building. No dead, no wounded. These men were more formidable than anticipated. It was time to try something different. After all, he had many children to choose from.

2

"Nightstalker Incorporated. How may I direct your call?" Jenna said in a smooth contralto voice. Her nose wrinkled in distaste as we approached. The smell of cordite and vampire ash didn't agree with her. You'd think she'd get used to it. As I headed around the reception desk, she absently handed me my phone messages while listening to whoever was on the other end of the line.

We all went our separate ways as we headed down the hallway behind the reception desk. Most of the Dreadnoughts headed to the locker room to shower and change. Dreadnoughts is the name of my personal team. Dale's Dreadnoughts. I thought it was kind of stupid myself, but my guys liked it, so I let it stick.

I took my messages and headed back to my office. Well, one of my offices. I had the fancy one with the big oak desk that I sat behind when I was forced to talk to clients and whatnot. The office I headed to was the one where the work actually got done. It was smaller and had your average Formica-topped office desk with a squeaky office chair behind it. A couple of dusty pictures hung on the wall. Some were of my buddies from back in the Corps. The newer ones were of my current group of guys. They were taken while we were out on a "business retreat". That's corporate talk for a week spent in Baja filled with cervezas, senoritas, and some really big fish caught out in the Pacific. In this line of work, you had to find time to blow off some steam.

I only had one picture on my desk. A beautiful slender goddess was holding a little girl that could have grown up to be even more beautiful than her mother. I don't want to talk about it.

The muscles around my eyes tightened as I stared at the picture on the desk. I was about to get all maudlin and depressed when there was a tap on my office door.

"Come in," I grumbled as I shook my head to clear it.

Smoke came walking nonchalantly through the door. "Hey boss, how'd it go?" He asked as he sat down across the desk from me.

"The usual as far as the operation, unusual as far as the target," I replied.

"I know right? Two babies in a week. That has to be on purpose." He said as his brow furrowed in speculation.

He was right about that. The vamps usually policed themselves. Anyone going around making uncontrolled children usually ended up as a pile of dust.

Smoke didn't look like a tech geek. He looked like a linebacker for the Bears. Nobody would've given him a second glance if he was packing a Saiga and punching out evil with my team. It was a role he'd filled in the past even.

In Smoke's case though it's a bit like beating a werewolf to death with a computer. It might get the job done, but there are a lot better uses for that computer.

Smoke kept all our guns and equipment in top condition. That's how he got his nickname. The smell of gunsmoke seemed to cling to him like a miasma.

He also kept us on the cutting edge of technology. If there was a bigger, better way to kill the monsters or keep us safe, from our trusty Saigas to small thermite grenades that were handy for burning up undead. Smoke was all over it. The noise-cancelling earpieces on our comm equipment were a godsend. Another item to thank Smoke for.

"I think I need to have a talk with Siobhan," I said with a scowl.

Smoke winced in sympathy. "I wonder how long it will be before she gets offended by your repeated refusals to dance the horizontal mambo with her."

I was flipping through my messages while he was talking and held up one between two fingers. "I hope at least once more," I said, indicating the message with a nod of my head. She wants to meet me at Tango's tonight."

Tango's was a high-end dance club, owned by Siobhan's family. It was popular enough that her people stayed well fed off the patrons without anyone dying. Vamps were so tricky, most didn't even know they'd been fed on. As long as they didn't kill anyone, the powers that be, had a hands-off policy towards the families. A policy that was well lubricated with many dollars, no doubt.

"Fun, fun," said Smoke as he started to rise from his chair.

"Hey," I said as he turned to leave. "Can you put a silencer on a Saiga?" I asked.

Smoke started to laugh until he looked back at me and saw the serious expression on my face. He turned back around and put his hand to his jaw in thought. 'You'll never make them silent." He said consideringly. "But you might bring the noise down to a dull roar."

I nodded at the qualifier. "Alex was complaining about the noise we made. Something about World War 3 is starting."

Smoke nodded as he headed out the door once more. "I'll see what I can do."

++++

It was still early enough that I could make it down to Tango's before it closed, so I headed to the locker room and took a quick shower. Once I smelled like a human again, I put on some casual street clothes and headed out to the parking garage. I stopped briefly to smile as my eyes roved over my baby.

She was a 1969 Mustang Mach 1. There was a 428 Super Cobra Jet engine under the hood and when I opened the throttle the gas gauge dropped almost as fast as the speedometer rose. I loved her, though. She was shiny, black and badass.

I cruised through the Chicago night. The Mustang's low rumble played counterpoint to AC/DC on the radio. The car and the music helped me get my head straight before I had to deal with Siobhan. She wasn't bad as far as vampires go really. She followed the rules, and so did her family. She just wasn't used to not getting her own way. What she wanted from me, I just couldn't give...Yet.

I rumbled up to the valet parking in front of Tango's. A young man with wide eyes came around the front to take the keys and give me a receipt. "Anything bad happens to her, it happens to you." I growled.

"Y..Yes, sir!" Replied the kid as he got into the driver's seat. Even after I put the fear of god in him, he was still grinning. I couldn't hold that against him.

The guy at the door was big, not as big as Petey, but he was still freaking huge. He was also a vampire. That was unusual. This place had human flunkies for that usually. As I drew close, our eyes met briefly before I dropped my gaze to his chest. I knew better than to meet a vamp's gaze for too long. You were just asking to get rolled if you did. "Rolled" is our term for mesmerized, by the way.

A beefy hand came up in a halting motion as I got within arms reach. "We're full." He said tersely in a gruff baritone.

I let my gaze come up, and I focused on the bridge of his nose. "Siobhan wants to see me," I said calmly.

"I don't care who wants to see you. Get lost." He said, throwing his shoulders back and his chest out.

I just sighed and reached into my pocket for my cell phone. Looking back up at him, I calmly dialed a set of numbers. I gave him a grin that didn't reach my eyes as the phone started ringing.

"Dale, what a pleasant surprise." Replied a sultry voice from the other end.

"Hey Siobhan, you've got some brainless slab of beef out on the front door that doesn't think I should come in and talk with you," I said. It was fun to watch the guy's expression go from arrogant to panic when his vampire hearing picked up Siobhan's voice. Not a lot of people have Siobhan's private number after all.

We both heard Siobhan's irritated sigh. "Marco, if Mr. Frost is not in my office in three minutes, you and I will be having a...discussion." Marco turned pale, well paler. They're all pale. He quickly unclasped the velvet rope and motioned me inside with a shaky hand.

The front doors opened into a foyer. On the opposite side of the large room, heavy double doors muffled the sound of the thumping bass coming from the dance floor. Another large vampire stood by the doors, looking at me warily, but not doing anything stupid. On the other side of the doors stood a small podium. A pleasantly smiling young lady stood behind it and made eye contact with me as I approached.

"Mr. Frost?" She asked in a sweet voice.

I nodded once, and she motioned me to a single door off to the side. She proceeded me to the entrance and used a keypad to open it. "Please follow me. Ms. O'Malley will see you in her office." She said as she led me down a long hallway covered in a plush, ice blue carpeting with understated artwork on the walls. At the far end of the hall, she knocked quietly on the door before opening the door and waving me through.

"Dale, how nice to see you." Said Siobhan as she rounded a desk, meeting me in the center of the room. She reached up and quickly hugged me, making sure she pressed every curve into me. Damn, she had a lot of curves. I hugged her back briefly before moving back. "We need to talk Siobhan," I said gravely.

"Straight to business Dale? You're no fun." Said Siobhan with a pout on her full red lips.

"Someone's making babies in your territory and leaving them to run wild. I'm starting to get tired of cleaning up your messes."

"It's not my mess Dale. None of my people would do this." She said, the temperature in the room cooling considerably at her words.

"You know better Siobhan." I shot back. "Either one of your family is doing it, or you've got someone trying to make a move on you by creating distractions. Either way, it's your mess."

Siobhan's eye's flashed in anger, and for a moment I wondered if I'd pushed just a little too hard. She glared at me for a moment, but finally sighed and nodded her head. "I fear you're right, but for love of the darkness I can't figure out who."

"No threats? No dirty politics?" I asked, one eyebrow trying to crawl up my forehead.

"Nothing unusual." Said Siobhan walking over to a small bar and pouring amber liquid into two tumblers. She swayed back over and handed me a glass.

The sweet, smoky goodness of a top notch Irish whiskey slid down my throat. "New vampires don't just get left alone in office buildings for no reason," I said after swallowing the amber elixir.

Siobhan sighed and nodded her head. "I agree, but none of my people are involved." She said in a troubled voice. "There is an unknown player, and we're not sure what they want."

"I didn't think there could be a vampire in this city that you didn't know about," I said, honestly confused.

"Up to last week, I wouldn't have thought it possible." She said with a troubled expression. "I have enough contacts around the city that I would have known if any outsiders were here without paying proper respect."

I nodded my head in agreement. Siobhan looked like sex on a stick, but she knew her business. She'd been at it for hundreds of years after all. "Any ideas how they're getting away with it?" I asked.

She shook her head and eyed me seriously. "It's almost like whoever made those children didn't have any regard for them. It's as if they were made by another youngster that didn't know what they were doing or...." she trailed off shaking her head again.

"Or what?" I asked gently.

She looked up at me with an uncertain expression on her face. It made her look vulnerable and adorable. The protective side of my inner caveman started to rise up. Of course feeling protective of a being who could snap me in half like a twig wasn't exactly rational, but then again, neither was my inner caveman.

"Or someone who isn't a vampire has figured out how to make them," she said, taking a deep breath. "I know that sounds impossible, but someone had to make the first of us."

I'd never really gone into the history of monsters. I'd learned enough to know how to kill them while having half a chance to stay alive in the process. "You don't know how your race started?" I asked in puzzlement. "I figured there was a few of you still around that remembered the event."

"Do humans know where they came from?" she asked with a sardonic smile. "We have our various origin stories, just like humans do with their stories of Adam and Eve or evolution, but like humans, vampires don't have factual evidence for any of them."

I could see her point. I had my own faith; you almost had to when you were in my line of work. There were enough other stories running around, however, that someone looking in from the outside would be hard pressed to know what to believe. "Well, keep in touch if you hear anything. I'll try to do the same." I said, preparing to leave. I thought

Siobhan was troubled enough that I could get out of there without having to defend my virtue. I was wrong.

"I like keeping in touch." She purred as she stepped deep into my personal space and wrapped her arms around my neck.

My hands came up to her waist, and I tried to push her back, but if a vamp doesn't want to let go of you, there's damn little you can do about it shy of staking them. Since I wanted to be alive when I left this place, staking wasn't an option.

"Dale, how long will you pine for what you've lost? I'm right here." She said softly.

This was a side of Siobhan that I hadn't seen before. In the past, all she'd done was throw blatant sexuality at me. Actually acting like she cared for my feelings was something new. I didn't trust it.

Reaching up I grasped her wrists, and she let me pull her arms from around my neck. "It's not time," I said with a rasp in my voice.

She looked deeply into my eyes for a moment before standing on tiptoes and kissing me on the cheek. "I can see that." She said as she backed away. "Don't wait too long," she said seriously.

3

Boom, boom, boom! The three round burst from Charlie's M16 didn't even make it flinch. Dust flew off the creature's chest to swirl in the beam emitted by the flashlight on Charlie's weapon. Small holes appeared in its chest like he was shooting a piece of old leather. I guess he was, kinda. The monster looked like a man with leathery brown skin stretched over sinew and bone. It looked like one of those mummies that you see on the Discovery Channel without the bandages like in the old movies. The fucker was fast too.

It had already taken down Jones and Akron. Stepping out from behind an old stone statue, it touched both of them on the shoulder. Their limbs immediately seized up, and they fell over like they'd been turned to stone. Charlie reacted first and managed to get off that burst into the thing's chest. All it did was make him the next target. The monster moved so fast it almost blurred in the dusty beams of the squad's lights as it crossed the intervening space. A clawed hand came arcing around, and it took Charlie's throat out with one swipe.

Conner and Murdoch opened up from across the room before I could get turned around. Two M16's on full auto seemed to have a little effect, but not much. It twitched and danced as the guys emptied their mags, but the monster, a ghoul, I would find out later, was already within reach and attacking before they could drop their mags to reload.

I was standing next to this big stone crypt. It was probably four feet wide by eight feet long. Faded engravings covered the entire thing. Right in the center, at the head of the crypt, the image of some demonic face was etched into the stone, screaming in rage at whoever looked at it. It was creepy as hell.

 I'd just put a gold necklace and pendant that I found in a little coffer beside the crypt, around my neck and turned to show off my prize when the monster struck. Before I could comprehend the situation, much less move, the ghoul had Murdoch down, blood gushing from his neck. It had a clawed fist wrapped around Connor's throat. It was pulling him in close, and his mouth was opening wider than it should have been capable of. Huge fangs extended from the mouth as it opened, preparing to bite a huge chunk right out of Connor's face.

The only good thing I can say about myself from that day was that I didn't lose my cool. I was a thieving, cowardly piece of shit who got my squad killed but I didn't panic. My M16 came up, and I put an aimed shot through the side of the ghoul's head, trying to distract it at least from killing Connor. It worked for about half a second.

The ghoul's head whipped around to glare at me. It's eyes seem to glow in the beam of my light as its evil gaze met mine. It seemed to take great pleasure in watching my reaction as it crushed Connor's throat in its clenched fist. Fear and panic overtook me as its eyes penetrated into my skull and stirred my lizard hindbrain into action.

Scrambling backward down the tunnel towards the entrance, I kept firing single shots as I went. It seemed to slow the ghoul down enough for me to keep space between us. The tunnel lightened as I got closer to the entrance and the ghoul's approach slowed. Holding up a taloned hand, it tried to shield its eyes from the encroaching sun. It came to a complete stop, hissing in fury as I reached the entrance. It's fanged jaws made loud popping noises at it snapped them repeatedly in frustration.

My pounding heart and trembling hand kept calling me a coward as I grabbed a grenade and pulled the pin. There were no ironic quips or bold statements as I tossed the grenade down the tunnel. I just ducked around the corner of the entrance and crouched down, covering my ears. When the grenade exploded, I woke up.

I sat bolt upright in bed, gasping for breath. I was drenched in sweat, and my heart thudded against my ribcage as my eyes darted around the bedroom, looking for threats that weren't there. My heart rate eventually slowed, and I ran a hand through my short salt and pepper hair. Looking over, I checked the time on my alarm clock. 4:23 am. Damn

Too early to get up, too late to go back to sleep. Sighing, I chose the first option and dragged my ass out of bed and into the shower. Yeah, I'd have to shower again after my run, but getting the stink of fear off me was an imperative.

The hot water from the shower soothed the knots from my back as I contemplated my nightmare. I'd had that same one so often now that it was almost like an old friend. There were worse ones hanging out in the depths of my subconscious.

This one had actually happened. It was how I found out that monsters really did exist. The official report said I was delusional from PTSD after an encounter with elements of the Iraqi military hiding in that cave. I disagreed hard enough that I was discharged from Uncle Sam's Misguided Children and told by a Colonel with a stern face not to talk about it or they'd find a deep dark hole for me. He also gave me a card and told me to call the number on it when I got back to the states.

My hand came up and grasped the amulet on my chest. The same one I had found next to that crypt. I'd worn it next to my skin ever since I got out of the caves in order to keep the memory of my squadmates fresh and alive inside me. It had the heavy weight of gold and the screaming demon visage from the crypt was also engraved on the amulet. There were writings engraved on the back, but searching the internet hadn't come up with anything like it. Shrugging, I dropped the amulet back to its spot over my heart and finished my shower.

A long run and a second shower put my head back on straight. By the time I got to the office, the sun had come up, and I was looking forward to a day of paperwork and training exercises. Not so much the paperwork part, but I liked the money it put into my bank account.

It turns out that all those conspiracy theorists are right, the government does know all about monsters. At least parts of it do. Their response is to pay people like my team and me to handle situations as they come up. The card that Colonel back in Iraq gave me was the contact for the bureau that wrote the checks.

That's how I got started in this business. The people on the other end of the line already knew about me. The were the ones that would have that unpleasant conversation with me if I started spouting off about what I'd seen. After verifying my service record so they knew I could handle the cool toys, it was just a matter of some paperwork. All the sudden, I was a monster hunter.

I was also very lucky to survive my first bounty. I think the Bureau does that on purpose to weed out troublemakers. The situations don't come up very often, to be honest since for the most part, the monsters police themselves.

Yup, it turns out that the scariest monsters of them all are mankind. The last thing the monster community, as a whole, wants to do is wake that monster up. People might be individually weaker, but there was a hell of a lot of us. Added to that, imaginations that excelled at finding new and better ways to kill things and you had a recipe for monster extinction.

Of course, just like people, there were monsters who didn't have a very firm grip on reality. They had their share of egomaniacs contemplating world domination, and brainless morons bent on destruction, just like we humans do. Occasionally, however, one of them slips through the cracks and starts to cause trouble. If the monsters can't handle the trouble without drawing even more, unwanted attention to themselves, then people like me get called in to take care of things.

I'm not sure why the government didn't have a monster hunting agency of its own. Theories abound. Some said that there just weren't enough monster attacks to warrant its own agency. Some said that the monsters ran the government and didn't want to be found out by some nosy bureaucrat.

I figured it was somewhere in between. I mean, have you seen John Kerry? If he's not a vampire, I'll eat my hat. Terrible disguise.

Anyway, if something big and bad got out in public, I or someone like me got a call. The hours sucked. Mostly at night as you might guess. Your life expectancy shortened considerably, but it was never boring, and the paychecks could run into six figures.

A couple hours of paperwork was all I could stand before the overwhelming need to shoot something finally got the better of me. Jumping on the elevator, I hit the button for the basement. Nightstalker Inc. owned the ten story building outright. We rented the top eight floors to local businesses and kept the bottom two as well as the basement for our own use. The basement was where we kept the armory and the shooting range. Extensive remodeling and soundproofing are insurance that a small war could kick off in that basement without the pedestrians walking by outside ever having a clue.

I heard the reports of automatic shotguns firing precision bursts over at the kill house. Someone was practicing tight quarters combat. Given our last job, that was a good idea. As I meandered that direction the firing stopped and my Dreadnoughts came trooping out the door.

Leading the pack was Lori, my team second. Rumor had it she'd won a beauty pageant in her younger days and looking at her; it was easy to believe. She was soft spoken with warm brown eyes. She had a smile for everyone unless you happened to be a monster. Then those eyes burned hot. The last thing many of them had seen before the end were those brown eyes staring at them over the barrel of a 23 gauge.

We met when a half-assed necromancer I was tracking raised three zombies. I say half-assed because he immediately lost control of them and was promptly eaten. Afflicted with constant raging hunger the trio, like all zombies, had made their way to a local park. The laughter of little kids drew them like a magnet. All that saved those kids was Lori standing between them and the zombies armed with nothing more than a folding lawn chair and an aluminum softball bat. Don't laugh. The only way to kill a zombie is by destroying the brain. She'd already put down two by the time I got there.

The rest of the team filed out behind her. Jake and Tommy were both former Special Forces. Ray was a former jarhead like me. Monica, or Money to her friends, was former Chicago Swat. John, and of course, Petey were just really tough guys who'd seen things that humans shouldn't see and survived to tell the tale.

Lori took off her helmet and safety glasses before giving me the nod. "How's it goin' boss?" she asked coming to a stop in front of me.

"Good," I said. "How'd it go in there?" I asked, nodding my head towards the kill house."

"Smooth as butter, just like always," she said with a grin. "You gonna take a run with us?"

"That's the plan," I replied. "I have an overwhelming need to kill something. Even if it's fake."

Lori raised an eyebrow at that. "Rough night?"

Lori knew about the nightmares; she'd been hunting with me long enough that she'd helped kill some of the sources personally. "The usual," I said, shrugging my shoulders.

"Siobhan have anything enlightening to say?" She asked with a quirk of her lip as the rest of the team drew around us.

"She swears she doesn't know the source," I said with a shake of my head. "She thinks there's a new player in town."

"Bullshit." Said Jake shaking his head. "She know's everything that moves in this town, right down to the cockroaches.

"Usually I'd agree, but something has her spooked," I replied, my brow furrowing into a scowl. "And if something has her spooked, we better be on our toes, boys and girls," I said, nodding once again to the kill house.

The next few hours were filled with gunsmoke as we ran various scenarios and talked about tactics. We also took the time to work out with our personal firearms, blades and other self-defense gadgets that Smoke had come up with.

All of us carried at least a decent sized combat knife around with us. Not so much for actual combat, but to take the head of anything that we could persuade to hold still long enough. You might not think that decapitation was possible with a knife, but those ISIS fuckers had proved that it was not only possible but effective if you knew the proper technique. ISIS, now there's a group of monsters I'd cheerfully take the bounty on.

 The gadgets that Smoke had come up with were things that would help you get away from a situation, so you could call in some firepower to put it down permanently.

Our version of pepper spray was a good example. It not only had high concentration capsaicin in it like bear spray, but it also had colloidal silver. Simple, but an amazingly effective deterrent when sprayed in the face of the various lycanthrope species. We usually tried to take lycans alive, since most incidents involving them were caused by accidental infection. If we could restrain them and get in touch with the local pack, there was a chance that we'd just have another productive member of society running around who just happened to get furry once a month. It was more dangerous to capture than kill, but it was a lot easier to live with yourself afterward.

We also had high amperage tasers that were effective if you had to go one on one with pretty much any monster while you were in your street clothes. Most things with a physical body conducted electricity fairly well and our tasers had enough kick to scramble the nervous systems of even the undead. At least for a few seconds.

Tazing, then running as fast as you could in the opposite direction was your best chance at survival in that instance.

Each of us carried our own personal arsenal around wherever we went. It varied from person to person, but we practiced diligently with what we carried as well as with what everybody else carried. You never knew when you'd have to take up a weapon from a fallen comrade to save everyone else.

My own kit consisted of a .45 Kimber 1911A1. It was a venerable old model, but it was reliable and threw big bullets. The bullets were hollow points with a frangible silver bead set into the hollow. I haven't come across anything yet that wasn't damaged at least a little by the combination. My blade was the trusty old K-Bar from my marine days. It was heavy, rugged and reliable. I didn't typically carry around any of Smoke's gadgets, but I had them in the glove compartment of the Mustang.

I'd just dropped the empty mag out of my 1911 when Smoke came in carrying one of the Saigas. He smiled at me and pointed to a large aluminum cylinder that was attached to the end of the barrel. Apparently, he'd been working on the suppressor idea. I took off my earmuffs and approached as he laid the shotgun down on the shooters table and unloaded several mags from a satchel he was carrying.

"Does it work?" I asked, gesturing to the foot long cylinder.

"We're about to find out." He said as he seated a mag and pulled back the bolt to set a round in the chamber. He shouldered the weapon and kicked off the safety before putting a three round burst down range.

It was still loud, but it wasn't as loud. A sharp crack issued from the weapon as each round of silver BBs and double ought buckshot made its way out of the smoking barrel. It was much quieter than the loud boom I'd come to associate with the fully automatic shotguns.

The rest of the team ambled over to watch the demonstration. Then of course, we all had to try it out. The weapon ended up getting a very thorough workout. It performed with the usual reliability of a Saiga. I wasn't sure about the added length and weight added onto the end of the unit, but it was a start.

By mutual consensus, we called it a day and decided to head out to Smitty's for a post training day libation. Hard work and the smell of cordite had done wonders for my stress level, but I still had

an itchy spot between my shoulder blades, like
someone or something had its sights on me.

4

The moon was just peeking over the eastern horizon as a deep voice started chanting in a language that had died centuries ago. Its pale silver light revealed row after row of headstones and grave markers. The words took on a sinister edge as they rolled from his lips.

His eye's widened in glee as he felt the ancient power rise within him. It had been ages since he'd tried such a spell. He had been held captive for so long. He was a shade of himself with little power left when his tomb had cracked, destroying the enchantments binding him. He'd been forced to feed on the life force of rats and other vermin just to gain enough power to ooze out into the night.

The days that followed had been torture. He'd hid during the day. The scorching desert sun forcing him to seek shelter in any crack or hole he could find. The vermin of those shadowed places sustained him as he continued to follow the trail of the artifact.

That precious piece of gold had nearly cost him everything. He'd planned long in its creation. It would allow him to control any number of undead without sapping his personal power With it he would control the world. His undead armies would crush those of man, and their deaths would give him more fodder to increase the size of his horde. Eventually, all would serve him, willingly and alive or undead as his slave.

His overwhelming arrogance made him incautious, however. Bitter self-recrimination tugged at him even now. He hadn't dreamed that anyone was powerful enough to disrupt his plans. The power of his spell, however, had drawn the attention of the priesthood and his wards had been insufficient to stop the combined might of the priests and the emperor's soldiers.

Their timing had been perfect. They'd descended on him in a pack while his power was at it's lowest ebb, drawn away by the nearly completed enchantment of the artifact. Nearly completed.

They couldn't kill him. He'd passed through that tattered veil long ago and returned with his soul safely hidden from man or god. The power of the priests was sufficient to entrap him, however. He was interred in a stone tomb, and the strongest of binding enchantments had been engraved onto all of its surfaces.

In a final effort to keep him in place, the priests had used some of his own magic against him. They used it to change one of their number into a ghoul. The volunteer was set to guarding the tomb for eternity, its strength and paralyzing touch stopping any who would dare to enter the tomb from freeing him.

The pain and thirst he felt as his power slowly drained over eons were a thousand times worse than crossing the great desert without water. Each second was exquisite agony as the final death tried to take him. Eventually, all that remained of his essence was a non-corporeal shade bound to this earth by a hidden reliquary containing his soul.

The undead guard had done his job well. The aura of fear that surrounded them had kept grave robbers away, and those strong enough to overcome the fear succumbed to its attack. He'd long since given up hope that he would ever see freedom. His surprise had been complete when an explosion cracked the tomb.

He refocused his attention back to the enchantment currently under way. The ground started to shake as the dead stirred to unlife. His power didn't reach as far as it once had, but he still managed to raise a dozen zombies to his cause. He could tell that the rest of the graves within his sphere of influence were simply skeletons and while also subject to his will, had insufficient power to defeat his intended victims and were thus, left behind.

The ground continued to shake as the creatures below, aided by his power, clawed their way to the surface. The earth over the graves bulged before the green sod cracked to reveal pale hands with torn nails, clawing their way to the surface. Arms and heads slowly appeared, covered in dirt and tattered clothing, his minions pulled themselves from their own graves.

Eventually, they all stood before him, jaws slack and shoulders slumped. He could feel their hunger trying to drive them on a search for the living flesh needed to sate the unending hunger inside of them. "Patience my children" soothed Ahriman, as he turned to lead them to the waiting freight truck outside the gates of the cemetery. "Soon you will have all the flesh you desire."

As the zombies trailed after him, two of his undead soldiers stayed behind and concealed themselves once more underground. These were more powerful with magical powers of their own. They would prove useful as a reserve...or an ambush.

++++

Something wasn't right. I looked around Smitty's and everything seemed fine. The Dreadnoughts were spread out across two tables in a corner close to the bar. Smitty himself was behind the bar. He was a grizzled old retired cop. He didn't know about things that go bump in the night, but he'd seen his share of horror.

I must have been brooding because Lori reached across the table and slugged me in the arm. "Hey," she said. "You look like someone kicked your puppy."

Shaking my head a little, I looked up and took a swig of my beer. "Something's not right," I said, staring off into the distance. "Feels like something nasty is headed our way."

The smile dropped immediately from Lori's face. "You gettin' one of those gut feelings again?" she asked, as concern painted her face.

Every once in awhile, I got these feelings deep down inside. Feelings that we were about to be dropped into a giant blender set on puree. It didn't always happen before something bad, but I'd gotten the feeling often enough over the years that Lori learned to look for the signs and take it seriously when I did. My gut had saved our lives more than once.

She sat up straight and stared at me hard. "Soon?" She asked.

The feeling was suddenly blooming up inside of me tinged with a sense of urgency you got when someone shouted "Incoming!" right before the RPG hit your humvee. "Yeah," I said. "Too soon."

I sat up straight, and my hand trailed to the grip of the .45 under my left arm as I looked around for the unknown threat. My guys went silent and on alert as they noticed my motion. Lori stood up and motioned over to Tommy. He was closest to the front door. "Check the front." She ordered curtly before turning her head to face Ray. "Ray, you check the back."

"What's going on?" Said Smitty in a gruff voice from behind the bar.

"Probably too much beer and not enough sleep," I said reassuringly as the rest of the team stood up.

Smitty wasn't buying it. He had instincts of his own, and he'd seen us all make movements towards the various weapons we all carried. "Don't mess up my bar Dale," he said in a growling tone as he moved to a spot by the cash register where I know he kept his old service piece.

I nodded in acknowledgment as my head seemed to turn of its own free will towards the swinging double doors that led to the back. Ray was about ten feet away from it when a pale form in a dirt encrusted suit from the '70's came through the door and immediately attacked a guy sitting in a corner with his girlfriend. The scent of rot and decay filled the air as more zombies streamed through the door, looking for a snack.

The guy's girlfriend screamed and fell back over her chair in a desperate bid to get away from the gruesome sight of her boyfriend being eaten. Her head smacked the edge of a table, and she lay dazed on the floor. Ray altered course and made a sprint for the girl. His M&P .40 appeared in hand as he tried to save her. He was the only one who could get a clear shot as the rest of the bar's patrons exploded in a riot of screaming and scrambling to get away from the creatures. I lost sight of him in the crowd, but the sharp crack of multiple shots told me he was putting his weapon to good use.

"Lori, get everyone out and cover the front!" I yelled as I reached down and grabbed the pedestal base of the small table Lori and I had been sitting at. I pushed the table top out ahead of me, using it as an improvised shield. I knew it wasn't going to be enough when I looked back to the fray and saw at least ten more zombies had entered the room.

"Petey, John, we need bigger shields!" I yelled as I pulled my .45 and started looking for a clean shot.

Petey and John tipped over a large rectangular table and picking it up, charged the small horde of undead.

Containment was the priority here. If the zombies got out and started biting everybody in sight, we could find ourselves fighting an army of undead instead of a dozen. My guys were the best though, and they knew their jobs, even if they didn't have their gear with them.

Petey and John dropped their table a few feet short of monsters shuffling towards them. They quickly knelt behind it and drew their sidearms. Ray dragged the screaming girl back several feet and dropped her, using his M&P to keep the dead guys at bay as he did it. Money came up on my six with her gun already in hand, using me as her shield bearer. Feeling her in position, I re-holstered my piece and put both hands on the table and started forward. Jake and Tommy were set up similarly to Money and me, except Tommy hadn't pulled a gun yet. They charged past Ray and the girl. Jake fended off zombies with his table while Tommy helped Ray drag the girl behind Petey and John.

The room cleared of patrons, and my guys were able to open up. The laser sight on Money's Beretta PS4 centered between the eyes of the zombie closest to us. A quick double tap took it down. My .45 could usually put down a zombie with one shot to the cranium, but with a 9mm it was best to use two rounds to make sure. I hoped she had spare clips.

The loud explosion of a .357 magnum told me Petey had put his Python into play. We gave him a hard time about carrying the old revolver, but there was no doubt that when he made a clean headshot, the zombies were going down for good.

Ray and Tommy got the girl to a safe place. Ray moved up between Petey and John. Tommy resumed his place behind Jake, putting a couple rounds into a female zombie dressed in what looked like something June Cleaver would have worn back in the day. Well, aside from the graveyard dirt, anyway.

The infectious bite that turns anyone into a zombie makes them scary as hell, but in the supernatural world, they're kind of the Homer Simpson of monsters. They come straight at you. Hunger drives all other thoughts from them. These guys were textbook at first. We fended them off with our makeshift shields and put several down in quick succession. Then something changed.

The zombies seemed to hesitate for a second; then all their attention focused on me. What the hell?

If it wasn't for the fact that a half dozen zombies all decided at once that I looked delicious, I would have said that our tactical position had improved. Their unified movement in my direction let the rest of the team focus on their shooting. Of course, the table I was using seemed to shrink into insignificance as the mass of undead bodies drew nearer.

Money dropped another zombie at the feet of its buddies with the final bullet in her magazine. "Shit," She said as the slide locked back. The rest of the zombies kept moving forward as Money desperately clawed for a spare magazine. The lead zombie still standing, shuffled forward and promptly tripped over the body Money had just dropped in front of them. We had some falling domino action at that point as a zombie impacted hard on my improvised shield, knocking it to the side. I took an involuntary step back, and my foot came down on one of Money's feet, sending us both crashing to the floor. Talk about a Keystone Cops moment. Sheesh!

Of course, the moment Money's ass connected with the barroom floor, the magazine she'd taken out to replace its empty companion, went flying out of her hand and went skittering underneath a stool that lay nearby.

The zombie mob saw their opportunity and rushed forward...and promptly fell over their buddies already lying on the ground. This wasn't exactly optimal for our situation as Money, and I were down there with them, and their heads had dropped out of the sightlines of the rest of my crew.

I reared back with my right leg and put a size 11 steel-toed boot into the face of the nearest zombie as he tried to grab me. It didn't do a lot of good because more hands were already trying to reach forward and pull me in. Piteous moans of hunger escaped them as they sought to bring anything living into their slavering maws.

One zombie that seemed a little sprier than his fellows lunged forward suddenly and I felt the crushing pressure on my ankle as his browned and rotten teeth bit down on the leather upper of my boot.

Panic took over for a moment as fear of becoming undead seized my mind. "Let go!" I shouted as I looked into the zombie's milky undead gaze. The funny thing there was that he did it. His mouth went slack, and he just stared at me for a half a second. Then most of the contents of his skull sprayed out the back of his head as the whipcrack boom of a high-velocity round being expelled from a handgun, sounded behind me.

Lori was reaching down with one hand to pull Money out of the way, so I could back up. Her other hand held the grip of her FN 5.7. The size of the rounds it shot was half the size of the rounds put out by my .45, but they made up for it with incredible velocity. The empty skull of the now still zombie proved that.

Lori's timely assistance allowed me to get clear in time for the rest of the crew to reacquire targets. In short order, the last of the undead stopped moving. Standing up, I looked around to make sure we were clear. I turned around and made eye contact with Lori, nodding my head in thanks. "Are we clear out front?" I asked

"All clear." She said with a concerned look on her face. "Several people with cell phones, though. Cops will be here any minute." she finished.

Nodding again, I pulled my own phone from my pocket. Amazingly enough, it still worked. I hit Alex's number on my speed dial. "You the one doing all the shooting at Smitty's he asked in a resigned tone."

"Yup, that would be us," I said as I motioned for the crew to clear the rest of the building. "Somehow a load of zombies popped up and came storming into the bar from the back," I said, doing a quick count of the bodies on the floor. "We've got twelve down and one dead civilian, who's going to get hungry and start moving again real soon."

"Crap," He said with quiet venom. "He doesn't have any bullet holes in him, does he?"

"No, we've avoided that so far," I said as my ears picked up the faint sounds of approaching sirens. "I hear your boys coming. You should probably give 'em a heads up."

"On it." He said, followed by the click as he disconnected.

"Okay boys and girls," I said, pulling my .45 from its holster and laying it on a convenient table. "Weapons down and hands up. I don't feel like getting shot by our boys in blue this evening."

There was a fairly loud clatter of hard steel implements of destruction being tossed down on various flat surfaces. We all raised our hands as we heard multiple police vehicles pull to the front of the building and cut their sirens. To my relief, they didn't charge in with guns drawn and barking orders. I was guessing that they were going to secure the perimeter and wait for the big guns. It's what I'd do.

Thinking about it for a minute, I dialed up Alex once more. "Now what?" came a curt response by way of salutation. I could hear traffic noises in the background, so I assumed he was on the way.

"Your boys are here, but they're not coming in yet. You got a leash on 'em right?" I asked.

"I put the word in." He said. "I'll be there in twenty minutes. Don't kill anybody!"

"We haven't killed anyone yet," I said evenly. "They were all dead when they got here."

"You know what I mean smartass," Alex said gruffly. "If another shot goes off you're gonna get company real fast."

"I hear ya," I replied. "We're waiting patiently."

As I clicked off with Alex, I turned to the crew. "Tie up the guy who got bitten before he starts moving. We do NOT want to have to fire any more shots or bad things will happen."

John and Petey were given directions to a roll of duct tape by an angry and shaken Smitty. He'd holed up under the bar while the shots were going off. "Dammit Dale!" He shouted angrily. That phrase made me think of that cartoon show, King of the Hill and poor old Hank Hill yelling at his stupid buddy. It wasn't exactly flattering.

"I thought I told you not to mess up my bar!" he continued. His hands were visibly shaking, but he was keeping it together pretty well so far.

"Sorry Smitty," I said with as much contrition as possible. "If we'd have been in full gear, we could have pushed them back outside, but we didn't have a lot to work with here."

Smitty just shook his head. "Who did you piss off and why are these guys dressed up as zombies? Some kind of new gang or something?"

I sighed at his question. Here came the part where I told him that the things that go bump in the night are real and that if he told anyone about it, the men in black would pay him a visit. It was never a happy conversation.

"They weren't dressed up like zombies Smitty. They were actually real life, well, real dead zombies. The question is, how the hell did they show up here? Did somebody build over an old cemetery or something?" I asked with a puzzled expression on my face.

Smitty stared at me with his mouth hanging open for a minute. "You're out of your ever loving mind if you actually think I'm going to believe that load of crap." He said finally.

"Look around you Smitty, what other answer can there be? You saw them start eating that poor fella over there." I said waving over to the corner where John and Petey just finished trussing up the deceased bar patron. "Cannibal gang freaks dressed as the undead is a better answer than just plain ol' zombies?"

Smitty tried to rally. His tough old cop instincts were telling him one thing, and the evidence was telling him another.

"Look Smitty," I said as gently as possible. "The police are going to spin this for media consumption anyway. Just go along with whatever they come up with and forget about what you actually saw. It's safer for everyone that way."

"Whadda ya' mean?" He slurred slightly as his brain continued to overload.

"It's pretty obvious the *Powers That Be* don't want Joe average to know about this stuff," I said seriously. "And if you go talking about it with people who don't know about it, they'll come have a very unpleasant conversation with you."

"You can't cover up something like this!" Smitty said, gesturing furiously at the mass of bodies on his floor. "People gotta know!"

"C'mon, you already know better than that. How long were you a cop?" I said sternly. "Tell me you haven't seen some shit that never made the evening news."

Smitty's eyebrows drew together as he contemplated what I asked. "B...But this is over the top." He muttered. "Nobody is going to believe this."

I pointed my index finger at him for emphasis. "Exactly," I said. "Nobody is going to believe this, so what do you think is gonna happen if you try to tell anyone about it?"

Smitty just stared at me again, his mouth trying to form words. Finally, his shoulder's slumped and he looked briefly to the floor. "Fuck," was all he said.

Lori walked over to him and put a consoling hand on his shoulder. "I know it's hard. I've been there." She reached into her pocket and handed him a card. "If you need to talk about it, give me a call. Heck, we've all been in your shoes. Feel free to talk to any of us. Just...keep it in the family, okay?" She finished with a look of sympathy on her face.

Smitty nodded absently as he stuffed the card in the breast pocket of his shirt. Lori patted his shoulder once more and turned to face me. "What's going on Dale? The way those zombies turned on you makes this feel personal all of the sudden."

I shook my head at her. "I have no idea," I said. "But you're right, this isn't normal, even for us."

My phone started ringing as we stared at each other in speculation, glancing down at the screen, I saw it was Alex. I pushed the 'accept' button and raised the phone to my ear. "Are you here?" I asked.

"Yeah, am I clear to come in?" he said shortly.

"Come ahead," I replied. "We're all disarmed and waiting like good little monster hunters."

Alex just snorted and clicked off.

"Okay, Dreadnoughts. Hands in the air for the boys in blue." I said as I raised my hands high.

We heard the front door open, and Alex's head made a quick appearance around the short wall that separated it from the rest of the bar. After assuring himself that he wasn't about to be eaten, he continued his entrance. A scowl was on his face as he took in the scene and all of the musty smelling bodies on the floor.

Seeing that we weren't about to be bum rushed by Chicago SWAT, we all put our hands down. "What the hell Dale?" Asked Alex. "Only you could attract zombies to a bar in the middle of a major city." He said, shaking his head and raising a radio to his lips. "Scene secure, hold perimeter until I get back to you." He said into the mic.

"Affirm" came the short reply.

"Okay, give me the story," he said, looking back up at me.

We rehashed what had happened. Each member of my crew pitched in to give his or her own account. Finally, he just shook his head. "But where did they come from?" He asked almost plaintively.

"Lori and I were just asking the same question when you got here," I replied. "So far, we don't have any answers."

He blew out a breath and nodded. "Well, I guess that's the first place to start." He stared hard at me for a second. "Do you think maybe Siobhan had anything to do with this?"

I looked at him in shock. "Why would you even ask that?" I said incredulously. "Vampires and zombies don't mix. At least not that I've ever seen."

He nodded at that. "Yeah, but she's powerful, and you've been blowing her off for awhile now. This seems to be targeted at you or your team."

"We've taken down a lot of big and bad," I said thoughtfully. "Maybe we got under something's skin. My gut's telling me it isn't Siobhan though."

"Are you sure it's your gut?" he asked with a raised eyebrow. "It could be something lower down that's making that call for you," he said with a lopsided grin.

"You know better than that," I said as my cheeks heated a little and some chuckles sounded from my guys. "I'll talk to her again, but I'm sure it's not her."

"Stevenson, sitrep!" came a voice from Alex's radio.

"I better get STAC in here before their heads explode." He said with a grimace.

STAC stands for Special Tactics. It's the unit that handles things like this. It was made up of people in the know, and they handled things when one of the specialist teams like mine were unavailable. They also handled cleanup and coverup. Usually, the coverup part went something like, "Gang related drug activity." You didn't think all those shootings in the Chicago area were due to their idiot gun control laws and real gang activity, did you?

For whatever reason, monster activity was highest in the midwest. It seemed especially concentrated in Chicago and St.Louis. That's why I set up our headquarters where I did. We were within driving distance of most of our bounties.

My Dreadnoughts raised their hands again, just to be safe, as the STAC unit made entry. I hate having guns pointed at me, but to their credit, STAC lowered them fairly quickly once they were sure things were well in hand.

Chris Taggart was the head of STAC. We'd crossed each other's path often enough that he recognized my team and me. He approached Alex and me, while surreptitiously looking at Smitty.

"Is he going to be a problem." He said, pointing a thumb in Smitty's direction.

"I don't think so," I replied. "I had *The Talk* with him. He's retired CPD, so he's handling it better than most."

Taggart grunted in acknowledgment and returned to directing his people.

We were forced to stand around until all the bodies were taken out in black plastic body bags. The coroner's office also had a special group for just such occasions. Finally, all the bodies were clear, and we were left standing with a forlorn Smitty, who was gazing sadly at the remains of his bar.

"Send me the bill for the damages Smitty," I said handing him a card. "The folks on that card are very good at cleaning up this kind of thing, and they don't ask too many questions." Smitty nodded at me absently as he stuck the card into his pocket, next to the one Lori had given him.

We gathered our weapons and finally got the chance to head home. My head hurt like hell as I pondered the ramifications of the evening's entertainment. Don't say it; I know I have an odd sense of what's entertaining.

++++

Ahriman howled in rage and beat his fist against the steering wheel of the big box truck. This *human* had defeated his children...*Again!* Worse even than that, his adversary had managed to wrest control of one of his children away from him. Clearly, the artifact was affecting this man. He continued to underestimate these people and their infernal technology. Before his imprisonment, it took magic and armies to stand against him. It was time to become more subtle perhaps. Instead of killing the man and his people outright, maybe he could convince him to turn over the artifact willingly.

5

I managed to drag my ass home far later than I had anticipated when I left this morning. Well, yesterday morning at this point. I turned around to close and lock the front door when my instincts finally managed to penetrate my sluggish brain and warn me that I wasn't alone. I continued on closing the door before turning around swiftly with a .45 filling my right hand. "I know you're there," I said quietly, and I scanned the darkness for movement. A shadow moved, over by my recliner and the reading lamp beside it suddenly came alight.

"You're awfully jumpy tonight Dale." Said Siobhan as she stood and walked with a sultry sway towards me.

"I'm tired Siobhan," I said as my eyebrows came together in a deep scowl. "What are you doing here?"

"I heard about the incident at the bar." She said as she came within arm's reach. Her hand came up and lay flat against my chest as she looked into my eyes. "I wanted to make sure you were alright."

It was a mark of how tired I was that I didn't drop my gaze immediately. Instead, I risked being compelled and looked deeply into the emerald depths of her regard. Something seemed to reach between us and try to enfold my will into a deep embrace, but then it just...slid away.

A look of mild consternation flashed across Siobhan's face, so fast that it barely registered. Almost instantly her smile was back in place. "Are you okay?" she said in a concerned voice.

"I'm fine," I said as I continued to stare down at her. A scent of high-end perfume underlaid by a hint of musk that didn't smell like a vampire at all tickled my sense of smell. It was intoxicating. I swear it was just the exhaustion that kept me from pushing her away as she stood on tiptoes to bring her lips to mine. Those soft full lips touching mine caused my eyes to close and my arms to surround her in a strong embrace. It was the exhaustion. I swear!

The hand Siobhan had placed on my chest earlier traveled down the muscles of my chest and abs. When it came to the bottom of my black t-shirt, it started gliding its way back up against the bare skin. I was starting to enjoy the sensation when her delicate fingers came in contact with the medallion around my neck.

My arms flew wide as she abruptly broke our embrace and stepped back hissing. Her eyes had turned blood red, and two-inch fangs descended from her lips. Instinct kicked in again and the .45 I still held in my right hand raised to point at the center of her forehead. We stared at each other for a brief moment, balanced on the edge of mayhem.

Slowly, Siobhan's fangs withdrew once more into her head, and she slowly regained control. "What the hell was that all about?" I managed to say with a voice that only shook a little.

"I apologize Dale." She said as her eyes slowly bled back to emerald green. "The power of your amulet took me by surprise. I've never felt anything like it." She said, her voice also having a quiver to it.

"What, this?" I said, reaching into the neck of my shirt and pulling out my medallion. "This is just some trinket I brought back from the sand box," I said absently.

"I think that it is much more than that." She said, eyeing it speculatively. "It has a great deal of power. The death of thousands imbues it."

I looked at the piece of gold around my neck closely. It was engraved with pictures and symbols that I had never been able to find a translation for. "That...makes sense," I said finally. "I found this in a tomb in Iraq. I've worn it ever since. I lost my men to what I now know to be a ghoul in that tomb."

Siobhan slowly approached me and looked at the medallion closely. "I can't read it, but it may be ancient Sumerian." She said as she continued to study it. "It calls to me," she whispered absently. "I think this may be why I am so...attracted to you," she said, meeting my gaze with a tremulous smile.

"Can you tell me anymore about it?" I asked. "Maybe give me a clue as to who made it?"

Siobhan's brow furrowed in thought as she continued to consider the medallion. "There are legends from that region that far predate my existence. Stories of great sorcerers who could create and control undead."

I snorted softly. "You mean necromancers?" I said incredulously. "I've yet to see one who could control more than three zombies, much less twelve like we saw tonight. None have even come close to raising something like a ghoul.

"Don't be so quick to discount them, Dale." She said seriously. "Times have changed, and a great deal of magic has been lost to the past. There are many stories of powerful Necromancers. Many of the vampire origin stories include mention of them.

My eyebrows rose at that. "I thought the origin stories related to Christianity. You know, Judas being cursed to walk the night forever for betraying Jesus? Things like that."

"Those are certainly the most popular legends among my kind. It could be because we can then trace our power back to the divine. However, there are other, older stories of vampires." She said contemplatively.

"What kind of stories?" I asked. I felt suddenly like a young history student sitting at the feet of some learned scholar.

"Long before the Egyptians and Romans dominated the world, the Persians were at their height. They made immense technological advances at the time. Some of their methods for moving water are still used today. Before the downfall of their society after the advent of Islam, they were also making great strides in their magical endeavors. It's believed that some of their ancient gods were actually powerful sorcerers from the different schools of magic. Necromancy was just one of them."

I considered what she said for a moment. "Does that mean this gives me the power to control the undead?" I asked after a moment.

Siobhan raised one eyebrow at me archly. "Why?" She said throatily. "Do you want to give me...commands?" Her smoldering look suddenly made me weak in the knees.

"Come here," I commanded abruptly, locking my gaze with hers. Her eyes widened a bit, but she stayed in place.

"I...I felt that!" she said in surprise. "It was almost like the compulsion we vampires use when we hunt. It's not enough to bend me to your will, but it may be able to control lesser undead."

My eyebrows tried to rise into my hairline at that. "I think I might have done that!" I said excitedly. "When we were fighting the zombies at the bar, I went down, and one of the zombies bit down on my boot." My face heated up as I remembered my panicked reaction. "Anyway," I continued as Siobhan's eye's widened slightly at my blush. "I kind of panicked and yelled at the thing to let me go...and it did. It just kind of raised its head up and stared at me."

"Dauntless Dale afraid of a little old zombie?" Asked Siobhan teasingly. My blush deepened a bit, but she continued on. "Can we do a quick experiment?" She asked seriously.

"What did you have in mind." I asked warily.

"I want you to take off the amulet and try to compel me again," she said. "I want to see if it is the amulet, or some inherent power of your own."

I hadn't taken the medallion off since that day in Iraq, so I was a little reluctant. It was good to make sure, though, so I reached up and slowly pulled the finely wrought golden chain over my head. I turned and set it on the table by the front door, where I left my keys at night. Straightening back up, I turned my gaze to Siobhan. I didn't feel any different, but I gave it my best shot.

"Come here." I said forcefully once again.

Siobhan actually seemed to lean towards me for a second. Of course, that could have been my imagination...or libido. She grinned after a moment then walked over to me once more. "I still felt a compulsion, but not as strongly." She reached up and wrapped her arms around my neck. "I came because you just sound so sexy when you're being all commanding like that." She cooed as she leaned in to kiss me once more.

I gently pushed her away after a moment. Damn, she was a good kisser. "That still doesn't explain who's coming after me, though. I said as I disengaged from her embrace.

Siobhan backed up with a devastating pout on her lips before sighing. "I don't know who exactly, but I do know that the zombie attack tonight was aimed directly at you."

"How do you know that?" I asked, my eyes narrowing suspiciously

"One of my people just happened to be on the roof of a building across the street from the bar." She said innocently. "He saw a freight truck pull up to the alley entrance of the bar. Imagine his surprise when the driver opened up the back doors of the truck, and a mass of zombies trooped out and walked directly in the back door of Smitty's."

"Just happened to be on the roof?" I questioned. "Siobhan, are you keeping tabs on me?" I asked gruffly.

Siobhan's eye grew wide, and her bottom lip quivered. "I worry about you, love. Your job is just, so dangerous." She said as she tried to hug me once more.

I intercepted her arms this time and stayed on task. *Yay me.* "Did your guy get a description of the driver, or maybe a license plate number?"

Siobhan shook her head. "He was too far away, and it was too dark for even one of my kind to make out," she said.

"This just doesn't make sense," I said in frustration as I absently reached down and put my medallion back on. "Who's powerful enough to raise a dozen zombies and control them well enough to put them in a truck and drive them across town?" I asked in frustration.

"Perhaps someone who wants their amulet back." She said, tapping the amulet with her polished nail through my t-shirt.

"I threw a grenade into the hole I found this thing in. It brought down the whole ceiling." I said, shaking my head.

"Never underestimate the power of the ancient dead, Dale," Siobhan said knowingly. "There are powers out there that not even one such as you can comprehend," she said solemnly.

"It was a long time ago," I said, almost plaintively. "Why is he just now coming for me?"

"You may have injured it when your grenade exploded," she said thoughtfully. "It may have needed all this time to recover and gain strength."

"Great" I said sarcastically. "You mean this thing might be getting stronger the longer it hangs around?"

"I wouldn't be surprised," she said. "My observer also mentioned that he could feel a presence from the driver of the truck. Almost as if he were being called."

"Wonderful," I said. "I need to get this guy, sooner rather than later."

"I need to get some sleep, Siobhan," I said looking down into her eyes once more.

"Indeed," she said with a mischievous smile on her face as she took my hand and tried to lead me off to the bedroom.

I held my ground and pulled back. She turned around and flowed into my arms like it was an invitation. Her smile dropped when I said "Alone." Her obvious look of sadness and disappointment twisted something deep in my core. "Look," I said with a sigh. "I care about you, alright? But I need to concentrate on getting whoever's coming after me before he succeeds."

Siobhan stood there for a moment, cradled in my arms before reaching up and kissing me lightly on the lips. "I will give you time," she said softly. "Be careful love." Then she was gone.

I stood there for a moment bemusedly before sighing and running my fingers through my hair. "I need a shower," I told myself as I head towards the bathroom. "A cold one."

"Daddy help! The bad man is coming!" Shrieked Emily. I felt like I was trying to run through quicksand and the hallway kept growing longer and longer. "Emily!" I bellowed in response. "Hold on sweetie! Daddy's coming!"

The tortuous run finally ended and I burst through the door of my daughter's bedroom. There was blood everywhere. The shell pink walls were streaked and splattered with it. The small bed with the frilly My Little Pony bedspread had a large puddle of it in the center. The teddy bear, thrown haphazardly on the floor was torn apart. More blood soaked the soft brown fur as if hands already drenched in blood had torn it apart.

My daughter was nowhere to be seen.

A terrible, soul tearing, scream echoed through the house. "Dale! God Help! Where are you? Why aren't you here?" The terrible screams and accusations continued as I ran as fast as I could through the ever-lengthening hall trying desperately to get to the master bedroom at its end.

The doorknob felt like ice as my hand grabbed and twisted it. I lunged in, eyes darting around the room for my pleading, screaming wife. Standing in the middle of the room was a creature made of shadows and darkness. Terrifying red eyes glowed out of the creature's head, and my wife and daughter were clutched in his massively clawed hands. Emily was limp in the monster's grasp, flopping around, like a rag doll.

Sam, my wife, was very much alive. She struck at the monster repeatedly, but her hands passed right through it. All the while she glared at me and screamed. "Why won't you help us! You should have been here!"

I was frozen in place. I couldn't move. I couldn't breathe. I stood in helpless terror as my wife was engulfed by the incredibly distended maw of the shadow creature. When she disappeared with one final scream of rage and terror, the creature looked up and met my gaze. I've never felt such hate and evil.

Abruptly the shadow monster moved. He lunged across the bedroom at me. I stood paralyzed, unable to move even a finger as his fanged maw engulfed me as it had Sam. Everything went black.

I landed on the floor beside the bed with a thump, fighting madly to escape the entangling blankets trying to suffocate me. With a roar of rage and loss, I finally tore them free and threw them across the room.

My body was soaked in sweat and my face was wet with tears. I sat huddled on the floor for a minute trying to recover. One sob managed to escape me as I rocked back and forth, staring at nothing.

That nightmare still happened too often. Okay, I guess I have to talk about it. I'd been out of the Corps for just over a year when it happened. I wasn't home to prevent it. I came home from the warehouse job I had working for a company that provided parts and machinery for the coal mining industry. I had to work late that cold November night. It was pitch black outside when I pulled into the driveway, and the headlights from my truck illuminated the front of the house and the front door, hanging half off its hinges.

The house was a disaster area. Furniture was overturned, the upholstery shredded. "Sammy, Em, where are you!" I screamed. The silence was the only answer. The police never found the bodies. All that remained was the blood, splashed and smeared all over Emily's bedroom. The coroner said that nothing could have survived that much blood loss.

The case was put down to a robbery gone wrong, possibly a druggie, high on PCP, looking for money to pay for his next score. I knew they were wrong.

I had seen claw marks on the walls, and PCP didn't explain why the bodies were missing.

That was the night I started hunting. I've been looking for the fucker that did it ever since.

I finally got myself pulled back together, at least as much as I ever am, and headed to the shower. The warm water was like a balm that soothed the tense muscles caused by my nightmare. Two cups of coffee while sitting in brooding silence at the kitchen table wasn't helping much, so I finally looked up at the clock on the wall. 9:27am. I told the team to take the day off before we parted company last night, but I figured there might be some paperwork or something at the office I could do to get my mind out of the dark alleys it had wandered down in the night.

Combat boots, jeans, and a black t-shirt. A black leather jacket that concealed the .45 under my shoulder well enough, and a pair of shades to cover my bloodshot eyes. I was ready to go.

The Mustang snarled awake as I turned the key and Twisted Sister was screaming out of the speakers about how they weren't gonna take it anymore. Perfect music for a commute through the streets of Chicago.

The office was quiet. Not much monster activity at 10:15 am on a Tuesday. I threw a half-assed wave at Jenna as I started around her desk towards the back. A delicate hand touched my sleeve, and I looked down at her. "You doing okay Dale? Heard you had a rough night. Even for you." She said with a sardonic smile.

I tried to return her smile. I'm not really sure if I pulled it off or not. Either way, Jenna understood. She was awesome that way. "I've definitely had better," I remarked. "Messages?"

She only had one slip of paper for me. Alex wanted me to call when I came up for air. No rush.

I got out my cell as I hit the office and pushed the button next to Alex's name. Thank god for modern technology because my memory for such things sucked. Trivial Pursuit, I was hell on wheels. Phone numbers and birthdays? Not so much.

The phone rang twice before Alex answered. "'Bout time you got in." He groused by way of greeting.

"It was a long night." I greeted back.

"I know, I was there." he said sarcastically.

"It got longer," I said tiredly. "Siobhan was at my place when I got home."

"Oh ho!" Said Alex enthusiastically. "Someone finally gets lucky?"

"Keep dreaming pa," I said shortly. "I managed to fight her off...again."

"How much longer you going to be able to hold out big man?" he asked seriously.

I sighed into the phone. "Honestly, I don't know," I said in a rare moment of candor.

"It's like that, huh?" he asked.

"Yeah, but I did get some interesting information out of her," I said, raising up out of my funk a little.

"Do tell." he responded

"Siobhan had somebody who just happened to be on top of a building across the street from the bar. Apparently, some guy pulled up in the alley and let a whole bunch of zombies out of the back," I said.

He whistled in surprise. "Well, that explains a few things." He said after a minute.

"Like what?" I asked.

"A cemetery across town was vandalized last night. The reporting officers were kinda wondering where the corpses had gone," he said with a hint of amusement. "I don't suppose this guy of Siobhan's got a license plate number, did he?"

"Too dark and too far away," I said in frustration. "All he said was that it was a freight truck."

"Okay," said Alex, "I'll check and see if any were stolen recently. Maybe that will give us a lead."

There was a brief pause then like Alex was collecting his thoughts. "It feels like someone's out to get you Dale," he finished solemnly.

"You're not the first or even the second to suggest that," I said with a sigh.

"Siobhan and who else?" He asked

"Lori may have remarked about it also," I said

"Did she ask about me after I left?" He asked hopefully. Alex has had a thing for Lori for years. Most guys did if they spent any amount of time around her. She seemed to have a black belt in romantic jiu jitsu, however. She deftly fended them off with a smile and a few kind words, leaving them wondering what hit them. Eventually, they would get over it and settle down to enjoy her friendship.

Not Alex though. I had to give him credit for determination anyway. "Not in your wildest dreams dude," I said trying to put a smile into my words. "She's so far out of your league that you're playing different sports."

"Yeah, you'll see. I'll wear her down eventually." He said confidently. "So who's trying to kill you and why?"

I wasn't sure I was ready to share about my medallion yet. I wasn't sure that having a piece of jewelry that let me control and possibly attract undead would go over too well in certain circles. "Who knows. I probably killed someone's pet zombie or something." I said, trying to sound casual

"Probably," Alex said with a snort. "I swear you could piss off somebody just by walking past them three blocks away.

"Did you check out the cemetery?" I asked, trying to change the subject.

"Yeah, not much to see. It was a pretty obvious zombie rising if you know what to look for. You know, pushed up dirt and bits of old wood right over the graves. I've never seen one that affected so many graves, though." He said wonderingly.

"Whoever raised them definitely seems to have more juice than your typical Necro," I said seriously. "I've never seen a zombie leave a meal to attack someone else. That's got to take some serious mojo."

"No doubt." Replied Alex. "Usually the necros don't have enough juice to control the one or two they managed to raise and the zombies end up doing our job for us."

"No such luck this time, it appears," I replied. "Let me know if you turn up anything on the freight truck. Otherwise, all we can do is stay on guard and wait for the next attack." I said in frustration.

"I'll keep in touch." replied Alex. "And Dale. Watch your back." He finished. I was actually a little touched by his concern.

"Will do. Thanks" I said as I clicked off.

After that, I went down to see what Smoke was up to. I found him in his workshop. Imagine if a computer lab and the local National Guard Depot got married. Their child would be Smoke's workshop. It was clean and organized, but it was just weird seeing computers and electronic components sharing space with various guns and other instruments of destruction.

"How's it going?" I asked as I walked through the door.

He didn't say anything at first, all his concentration focused on the job in front of him. Finally, he stepped back and turned around. "Good," he said with a smile. "Come check it out."

I walked up and stood beside him. Situated in the vice was one of the Saigas. A shorter version of the suppressor he'd been working on was mounted to the front. It was also blackened to match the rest of the gun. "I think we have a battle ready version now." He said proudly. "I shortened it and increased the amount of dampening material. It's a bit shorter but just a little bit bigger around. Should do the trick, I think."

"Nice," I said with a grin. "Do I get to play with it?"

"Sure," He said returning my grin. "Let's see what she'll do."

We decided to run the kill house. It would be a good test to see if the added length hindered movement significantly. The Saiga did its job admirably. The extra weight on the front end took some getting used to, but the POP, POP, sound it made was a big improvement over its usual cannon like BOOM.

"Go ahead and make up enough for everyone," I said with a smile. "This should appease Alex. At least a little bit. I'd like them as quick as you can safely do it too. If you don't mind."

"What's the rush?" asked Smoke with a raised eyebrow.

I told him about the conversation I'd just finished with Alex. "Something tells me we're going to be making a racket inside city limits again and probably sooner than we'd like."

Smoke nodded. "I can get three more made up by this evening," he said consideringly. "That'll give each Dreadnought shooter one to play with."

"Good enough, thanks," I said and headed back out.

The rest of the day was spent on doing paperwork and making phone calls. I called the team members, just to make sure they were doing okay and to let them know about what we were speculating on as to our new adversary. "So, watch your back," I said to each of them seriously. Of course, every time I said it, the response was something similar to. "Hell, as long as you're not around we should be fine." Assholes.

I'd just sat down in front of the TV with a hamburger and a cold brew when my phone rang. Looking at the screen, I saw Alex's name.

"Dammit, I just sat down to dinner." I said by way of greeting.

"Put it in the fridge for later," He promptly responded. "There's been another disturbance out at the cemetery. The caretaker said some freaked out druggie dressed as he lived in the '70's charged him as he was shutting the gate for the night."

"Charged him? You mean shuffled after him moaning don't you?" I said skeptically.

"The guy swears that it was running when it hit the fence. He said if he hadn't had the gate locked it would have gotten him."

"Alright, we're headed that way." I said with a sigh. "Keep everyone back. You know the drill."

"On it," he said as I clicked off.

I quickly sent a group text to the team and headed for the door.

The Mustang rumbled through the night at exactly four miles per hour over the speed limit. I didn't need the delay a speeding ticket would cost me, and I knew how far I could push it. Pulling into the underground parking garage, I could see that a couple of the Dreadnoughts were already there. Jake's old Jeep and Petey's lifted Ford F250 were already in their assigned spots.

I jogged over to the express elevator and punched in the security code that gave me access. Two minutes later I was in the locker room, putting on my tactical gear. Shucking my street clothes, I donned a pair of Fire Hose work pants. Tough and resistant were the name of the game. They were even water...or blood proof. A black Under Armour shirt came next followed by a heavy T-shirt. The extra layer helped stop the body armor I put on next from wearing holes in my delicate flesh.

The .45 went on one hip, and the K-bar went on the other before I reached in and pulled my newly suppressor accessorized Saiga from its spot in my locker.

By the time I was dressed everyone else was accounted for. Two minutes later the last of the stragglers (Tommy. He always seemed to be on a date when a call came in.) was dressed, and we headed for the team Suburbans.

I briefed the team over our comm units as the two big Chevy's cruised through the night. No, they weren't black. One was blue, and the other was maroon. Black Suburbans stick out like a sore thumb. Everyone thinks you're a gangbanger or a fed. Funny how those two groups have similar tastes in vehicles.

"According to Alex, the caretaker swears that the assailant charged him at a run," I said, summarizing. "He was probably just freaked, but assume the worst."

We pulled up outside the cemetery to find Alex standing beside his SUV.

"I haven't seen anything from here, but I wasn't about to go in by myself." He said as I approached.

"Wise of you," I said with a smile. "My boys and girls will check it out. You stay out here near a radio in case it's something worse than a couple of zombies."

"Sounds like a plan to me." He said, reaching in and grabbing a nice hot cup of coffee from the cup holder of his vehicle with a grin. Jerk.

We broke out the shields and formed up at the gate. Alex had retrieved the key from the maintenance guy and had it open for us.

We dropped our night vision goggles into place and formed up in a box formation. Petey and John led the way with shields ready. The other two shield guys, Ray and Jake, took up positions on the flanks. Money and Tommy hefted their newly suppressed Saigas and took up position behind Petey and John. Lori and I brought up the rear where we could backup our guys and cover the rear.

If we were fighting humans who might have guns, I would have used a more spread out formation so that we could maneuver, but when you deal with creatures that have to get within arm's length to do their damage, the close formation works better. Especially when you factor in the possibility of supernatural strength and speed.

Through the green glow of our NVGs, we could see a taped off section of the graveyard. Of course, it was back in the far corner. Bad guys never seem to do things right up front by the gate. It's really inconvenient.

The cemetery seemed fairly nice, lush grass surrounded the grave markers and trees of various sizes grew along the edge and were interspersed throughout the cemetery itself. We took a straight line towards the taped off section, scanning the night and checking behind any grave marker large enough to hide something nasty.

It took a few uneventful minutes to reach the site of the zombie summoning. When we reached the tape, I had the formation sidestepping along the perimeter keeping our focus on the disturbed mounds of earth. Apparently, I should have been focusing on the trees.

Our first indication of trouble was when a pale white body fell from the night to land on Money. The momentum carried both Money and the monster into Ray, and they all went down.

"Wight!" cried Lori urgently as she reached for her tomahawk, knowing we couldn't shoot the damned thing when it was in amongst us.

Crap, wights are nasty. They resemble the people they were in life, but with pale almost translucent skin that was way tougher than it had any right to be. Similar to ghouls, they also had a magical touch ability. The wights differ in that instead of a touch that paralyzes, like that of a ghoul, the wight's touch drains energy, leaving the victim exhausted and slow mentally. Some people can shake it off, but most just lay there and get eaten.

Team discipline and hours of practice saved our lives then because no sooner had the wight taken down Money when another one hit Jake's shield on our flank. The impact forced him back a step, but he retained his footing. The wight continued to scrabble and push at the shield, trying to get at the meaty goodness behind it. This gave me the time I needed to sidestep and get a clean shot at it as John pivoted 45 degrees and brought his shield around to cover Jake's left side.

A three round burst from my Saiga sent the creature sprawling to the grass, but it didn't stay there. I did mention how incredibly tough their skin is, right? The wight leaped to its feet and lunged to attack again. This time, John was the unlucky recipient of it's attention. Unfortunately, he wasn't able to keep his footing and went down with the wight landing on top of him and his shield.

We were so screwed. Both wights were in among us now, and that took the Saigas right out of the equation. I've never heard of anyone beating these bastards with blades and maybe handguns if we got just the right angle.

In a fraction of a second, my eyes took in the scene like a snapshot. Money was down and limp. The wight on top of her was scrambling to remove Lori's tomahawk from its shoulder. Ray was struggling to get up and into the action. His shield was still in his hand, and he was clawing at the pistol on his hip.

Petey was as reliable as the mountain he resembled. He continued to focus on his area of responsibility in case there were more of the bastards. Only occasionally would he flash a glance over his shoulder at the conflict behind him.

On the other side of the formation, John was also limp now, but the wights attention was focused back on Jake as he tried desperately to force the monster off his buddy, using his shield.

I started to reach for the .45 and my K-bar thinking all the while that we'd finally met our match. The faces of my wife and daughter flashed through my mind. Maybe I'd get to be with them again. Then, oddly Siobhan's face replaced them in my head. I flashed back to our conversation about my medallion and how I may be able to control lesser undead.

The prospect of imminent death can focus one's mind brilliantly. I threw everything I had into a command aimed at the two monsters amongst us. "*Stop!!*" I commanded thunderously. My eyes widened in amazement as they both paused and two sets of eyes shining sinisterly in the green light of my NVGs focused their attention on me. They stayed frozen for only a second, but at least now all their attention was on me instead of the team. Go me.

Both wights immediately started trying to get to me. That meant the wight on Money swung a vicious backhand at Lori that sent her sprawling. Petey and Ray were in no position to be of help. Any action they took with their shields would just push the monster towards me, and neither could shoot it without endangering one of the team. The wight on John tried to stop trying to eat him and refocused his attention on getting to me. He seemed to want to take the most direct route, which was right through Jake and his shield.

I redoubled my efforts in trying to use my new found magic or mental power, whatever you want to call it, to repel the wights. As I pushed harder and harder, I noticed a spot on my chest growing hot. The amulet! Acting on inspiration, I reached under my armor and t-shirt and exposed it to the night. As it thumped against my chest armor, I tried to focus everything I had through it and out to the wights.

It must have helped because the wights stopped once more. It was close, though. I could feel their presence in my soul, and I knew they were on the edge of breaking my tenuous control.

Anger started suffusing me as we engaged in our battle of wills. It roiled up from deep inside me . All the hate and pain creatures like these had caused me came to the front and fueled my will. Gathering the power, I pushed it all into one last desperate command. *"**Just DIE already!!**"* I shouted in rage.

The amulet on my chest flared brightly, illuminating the surrounding area in flash of white light that blanked out my NVG, blinding me temporarily. As quickly as it had come, the light dimmed until the amulet was just another shadow on my chest armor.

A wave of exhaustion overtook me and drove me to my knees. I was afraid my command had failed, and one of the wights had reached me. Blinking furiously, I tried to clear my vision of the spots that danced before my eyes. After a second I could make out the pale shapes of the wights lying motionless in the cemetery grass. Money and John were still down also. The rest of the team stood in a semi-circle around me. Looks of shock, surprise and maybe a little fear marked their expressions.

"What the hell was that?" muttered Tommy, his eyes wide with shock.

"I'll explain later. I promise." I said in an exhausted voice. "Right now, we need to see to Money and John. Petey, can you please remove the heads from these two. I don't want to take the chance they may just wake up."

Petey regarded me with a stoic expression on his face for a moment before nodding and reaching over his shoulder to retrieve his battle axe.

Lori was crouched over Money. "How is she?" I asked as I tried to struggle to my feet.

"She has a pulse, and I don't see any bleeding. That's about all I can tell you right now," she replied somberly.

I looked over to where John laid. Jake and Tommy both knelt beside him. "Same here boss," came Jake's voice from the darkness.

Several meaty *thunks* from Petey's axe later and we were headed back to the Suburbans, supporting our unconscious friends as best we could.

Alex ran over as we approached the cemetery gate. He stopped abruptly, taking in the sight of us carrying two of our own. "W...What the hell happened?" he asked in a shocked tone.

"Wights," I said curtly as I trudged tiredly along behind my guys. "Two of them."

"Oh, crap," said Alex, his face going pale. His eyes locked on the two limp forms of my Dreadnoughts. "Are they...?" he started.

"No" interrupted Lori as we got to the vehicles. "Just unconscious."

Alex nodded his head in relief. "Did you get the wights or do I need to get some backup over here?"

The team all seemed to be looking at me out of the corner of their eyes as I responded. "We got 'em. All we need is cleanup." I said tiredly.

"I only heard three shots," said Alex in puzzlement. "How'd you manage to kill two wights with only three shots"?

I pondered what to tell him for a few seconds as the team loaded up Money and John. "Come by the office after the cleanup crew is situated. I'll explain to everyone all at once."

Alex stared at me for a moment like he was going to complain, but the look on my face must have convinced him otherwise. "I'll be there in a little while."

I nodded my thanks and turned to Lori. "Can you call Doc Brown and have him meet us at the office. My gut's saying they'll recover, but we need to get them checked out."

She just nodded and pulled out her phone.

7

Ahriman staggered suddenly as he felt the magical life force imbued to his two children, snuffed out simultaneously. He'd felt the death of multitudes of his creations over the centuries, but to feel the existence of two powerful undead wink out in an instant, spoke of a powerful cleric. He did not think a priest of such power even existed in this age. That left only one culprit, the wearer of the amulet.

It seemed the power of this mortal was growing quickly. That, or he was beginning to understand the power of the amulet. That being the case, it became even more imperative that he recover his treasure as soon as possible.

He looked down at the two creations kneeling on the floor in front of him. The ghoul's he'd sent to retrieve the amulet had failed. They brought back the corpses as penance. It had been insufficient. He retrieved his power from the ghouls, rendering them instantly to dust. Almost as an afterthought, he infused the two corpses in front of him with the power he had retrieved. It healed the physical injuries and placed the corpses in a state of suspended animation. In this way, he'd been able to keep them in case of need. Waste not, want not, after all.

Ahriman congratulated himself on his forethought now. Since the power available to him in his weakened condition seemed insufficient to taking the amulet by force, He would use guile instead. It was time for man and wife to be reunited.

++++

"They'll live, but they're going to be out for awhile." Said the Doc, a couple of hours later. "The touch of a wight is serious business. It's going to take physical therapy and retraining to bring them back up to where they were."

I nodded in agreement. I'd heard of the wight's power. Not only did they suck the energy out of you, but they also seemed to drain your skills and abilities. It was probably going to take months of conditioning and tactical training before I could let them into the action again. "Thanks, Doc," I said, reaching out to shake his hand. "They'll get everything they need."

I watched him leave the ready room before turning to face the rest of my people. Alex was standing off to the side. All eyes were focused on me. Facial expressions ranged from tired to angry. Tommy started things off.

"What the hell boss? Humans can't control undead this side of a priest with serious mojo. You get religion all the sudden?" He asked in a puzzled tone.

I shook my head as I reached into my shirt and withdrew the amulet around my neck. I studied it briefly before letting it fall to rest outside my t-shirt. "You've all heard the story of how I got this. Apparently, it's more than just a bauble. According to Siobhan, It's a very powerful talisman, probably used by some ancient necromancer. It appears that it gives me a little ability to control undead."

"A little?" Said Tommy in exasperation. "Dude you put down two wights for the count. That's more than a little."

"Which brings up another point." Said Jake, anger clearly written on his face. "Why the hell did you put us in danger when you could have handled it all by your little self."

My anger rose to meet Jake's at his accusation. I stood up slowly and our eyes locked. "Do you really think I'd endanger the crew like that if I knew I had that ability? Do you honestly believe I wouldn't have said anything about it beforehand if I knew what kind of juice I had?" I said through gritted teeth.

Jake and I continued to eyeball each other for a few more seconds before Jake's eyes dropped to consider his shoelaces. "Naw, I guess not," he mumbled. "It was damned creepy though boss. I thought my eyes were playing tricks on me when you told that zombie in the bar to stop, and it obeyed you. I just shook it off. Then you not only command, but destroy not one, but two wights at the same time? I figured you had to be hiding something."

I nodded at Jake somberly. "I shook off the zombie thing too. I figured it was just a coincidence or something." I said with a sigh. "I was talking to Siobhan last night, though, and her fingers came in contact with the amulet. She said it was very powerful."

Lori put her hand on her face, trying to conceal a shit eating grin. A couple of titters sounded around the room. "Okay, what?" I asked in exasperation.

"Don't you keep that trinket under your shirt?" Lori asked with wide eyes. "What was Siobhan doing with her hand under your shirt Dale?

My face grew hot at the cheesy looks I was getting from the crew. Alex winked and nodded like he'd had a suspicion confirmed. "None of your business smartass." I had snorted at Lori before a chuckle escaped me. I was embarrassed about Siobhan and me, but I was also grateful that the tension level in the room had dropped back down to acceptable levels.

"So is that amulet the cause of the personal attacks?" Lori asked, her face becoming serious once more.

"That's what Siobhan thinks," I said in agreement. "She thinks we probably woke something up in that tomb in addition to the ghoul that killed my squad and it's just now coming around to get its necklace back."

Looks of bemusement clouded the faces around the room as everyone considered the situation. "One more thing," I said with some hesitation. "Apparently some of the amulet's mojo has rubbed off on me. I seem to have some power over the undead even without it on. At least that's what Siobhan says." I concluded.

Again with the snickers. "All undead? Or just a pretty Irish undead in particular?" Tommy said with a guffaw. "Lust ain't a superpower boss." He continued as the room started laughing uproariously at my expense.

I let the laughter continue for a moment or two before raising my hands for quiet. "Alright, now that you have that all out of your systems, back to business," I said with a stern glance around the room. "Everyone needs to be on guard at all times. It wouldn't surprise me if this thing tries to use one of you as bait, so be careful and try not to be alone. Just in case."

"Let 'em try," growled Tommy. He hurt two of our own. It's time for some payback."

A rumble of agreement sounded around the room. I nodded in agreement at the sentiment. "No lone wolf bullshit" I commanded as my boys and girls started to meander towards the exit. "Remember, we survive these supernatural fucks because we're the best damn hunter team on the planet, so get back up if you see anything suspicious." Another rumble of agreement sounded as the Dreadnoughts left the room.

"I'll look deeper into any mysterious deaths that occurred recently. Maybe I can spot a pattern," said Alex as he prepared to leave.

"Suspicious deaths in Chicago? Good luck with that." I said with a snort.

Alex just shrugged his shoulders. "It's worth a shot." He said before waving a hand over his shoulder and walking out of the room.

Once the crew went their separate ways, I went and sat in the room where John and Money lay unconscious. I sat quietly watching them breathe peacefully as I beat myself up inside. I couldn't help the feeling of guilt that crept over me. If I'd been just a little better, maybe if I had taken some time to experiment with this ability...My phone rang.

"Frost," quietly I said when I raised it to my ear.

"Stop beating yourself up." Said a soft feminine voice on the other end.

"What, you can read my mind now?" I asked Siobhan as I tiptoed out of the room.

"Let's just call it woman's intuition." I could almost see her ruby lips part in a smile

"Well, it's creepy. Knock it off." I said, but a small smile was forcing its way onto my expression.

"Never," she said with a throaty chuckle. I felt her become more serious as she continued. "I felt the magic on the air tonight. It was...bad" she sighed uncertainly.

"It could have been me," I said. "I had to use this new mojo to put down a couple of wights a little while ago.

"I heard the story," she said. She continued on quickly before I had the chance to ask just who in the hell had blabbed. "This was not from you. It was dark on a level I have seldom felt before."

"Could you tell what the magic was used for?" I asked, focusing back on the matter before us.

"It felt like a vampire creation, but...different." She said in a troubled voice. "It felt almost transformative. Like someone had created one of my kind from some other version of undead."

"Is that even possible?" I scoffed at the thought.

"Not that I know of.." She said a bit haughtily. Like I'd offended her a little by questioning her insight. "If this being that is after you is as old as we fear, however, he may have knowledge that's been long lost to the ages."

"Sorry," I said. "I didn't mean to second guess you. Just on edge, I guess. Can you pinpoint where this magic happened or where this new vampire is?"

"No, I couldn't.." She said with a sigh of frustration. "My people and I will endeavor to find what became of the creations, however."

"Thanks, Siobhan, I appreciate it," I said gratefully. "Keep me informed okay?"

"Of course." She replied. "Get some rest."

I clicked off and sat in the ready room thinking for awhile. Could this be the next volley in this creep's war against me? How can you transform one type of undead into another? How tough would it be to destroy such a creation?

My head started swirling around in circles with all the questions. I finally decided to take Siobhan's advice and get some rest. I hit the lobby on my way to the parking garage to find Lori and Jake sitting in a couple chairs in the waiting area. "Headed out boss?" Asked Lori as they stood up.

"Yeah," I said, looking at them quizzically. "What are you two still doing here?" I asked.

"You're the one who said not to be alone." Piped up Jake. "We figure that goes double for you since you're the one with the big bullseye on his chest." He said, nodding at the spot on my chest where the amulet lay hidden once more.

"I'll be fine," I said gruffly. "I'm the one with the magic mojo, remember?"

"Just the same, anything that can raise and control two wights and a dozen zombies, may be more than you can handle by yourself." Said Lori. "So like it or not, you get an escort home."

Seeing the stubborn looks on their faces, I knew there would be no dissuading them. They also happened to be right. I couldn't go all lone wolf after telling my people just the opposite. "Fine" I sighed. "But if we're going to do this, we may as well do it right. Let's suit up, so we can sweep the house when we get there. You guys can follow along in one of the suburbans, just in case we get hit enroute."

Twenty minutes later, My mustang led the armored suburban out of the parking garage and headed home.

The drive was blessedly uneventful. Clearing the house was also. It was good kill house practice, though. "See, I told you there was nothing to worry about." I said as we stood in the living room after the sweep. "Now, would you two please go home?"

"No way boss man." Said Jake "We got your back for the duration." Lori nodded her agreement.

I sighed and ran my fingers through my hair. "Come on guys. I'll be fine. I have the magic mojo and a Saiga." I said, hoisting the shotgun to prove my point." I'm plenty protected."

"So you're going to throw us out into the pitch black night without your protection?" Lori asked, putting on her best helpless little girl face. The face was somewhat marred by the impish smile she was trying to conceal, however. She knew she had me.

Shaking my head, I threw my hands in the air in defeat. "Fine, be that way. You know where the spare bedrooms are." I said as I turned and headed for my bedroom.

"Night boss" came twin voices, overflowing with satisfaction. My hand raised of its own volition as I strode down the hall, giving the middle finger salute. Laughter chased behind me as I closed the door.

++++

Sam ran her hand up and down my hairy forearm as I spooned her in close. The feeling of her wiggling against me as she found a comfortable spot was doing interesting things to me. She moaned softly as my hand moves up her torso to cup her breast while placing a soft kiss onto the nape of her neck. It was times like this when I felt the most contentment. The most beautiful woman in the world was snuggled next to me, and our daughter lay quietly in the next room, dreaming of unicorns and My Little Pony.

Rolling in my arms, Sam turned to place a soft kiss on my lips as she ran her hand through the hair on my chest. I ran my hand down the cool skin of her back as I returned the kiss with interest. My breathing became ragged as our passion is increased. I felt her lips pull into a smile as we continued to kiss, knowing the effect she was having on me. My hand reached the curve of her luscious posterior, and I grabbed it firmly and drew her in tight to me, my quickly hardening manhood rubbing against the cold skin of her pelvic mound. "Cold skin. Wait. What?" My subconscious mind knew this was all a dream and I sighed internally as I steeled myself for the nightmare to come.

Sam ground against me enthusiastically as her hand continued to explore my chest. Her trailing fingertips came in contact with the amulet where it was hanging down towards the bed. An instant sensation of heat and a flash of light brought me instantly awake. I held Sam tight as I looked around trying to detect the threat that I instinctively knew threatened my family. Seeing no immediate danger, I looked down at the taut form in my arms.

Sam, but...not, looked up into my eyes with a wicked grin on blood red lips. "Hey, lover." She said in a sultry voice.

It all came crashing down. My brain began to grind into motion as I stared muzzily into my dead wife's blood red gaze. Adrenalin surged through my body, and I pushed her violently away and rolled off the bed and onto my feet. "What the fuck?" I said in a hoarse gasp as I stared at the nude form of my wife still laying on our bed. "This must still be the nightmare," I muttered to myself.

"It's not a nightmare baby. I'm back." Said Samantha. "Ahriman freed me, so we could be a family again." Her eyes were slowly fading from red to their normal blue luster.

My brain was overwhelmed. The husband in me rejoiced to see my beautiful wife laying in our bed. The father in me immediately wondered if Emily was here too. The monster hunter knew what I truly faced, and the soldier in me reacted.

Taking a step back, I snatched the .45 off the bedside table and pointed it at the vampire on my bed. The sound of the safety clicking off was loud in the silence of our bedroom. "Who the hell are you? My wife is dead. Who's Ahriman?" I asked as my brain continued to try to get a grasp of the situation.

"It's me, baby. It's really me." The Sam vamp said. "Ahriman...he rescued us from the ghouls. He brought us back to life."

"Whoever you are, you are most definitely not alive," I said, staring at her over the sights of my gun.

"W...We were already gone when Ahriman found us. He did what he could." She said with a pleading quality to her voice. "He just wants us to be a family again."

"Oh really?" I snorted in derision. "What's he get out of this deal? Or are you telling me this necromancer of yours is all about altruism and the good of mankind."

Sam stared at me for a minute, as if trying to decide what would be safe to say. "You have something that he needs." She said, waving at the amulet laying on my chest. "He needs it to become his old self again. He's willing to trade." She said with a smile full of promise for the future.

The different sides of my character continued to war with each other. The husband continued to see his gorgeous wife and begged to return to her arms. Conversely, the monster hunter said Oh hell no. There's no way we help a powerful necromancer get even more powerful. She's already dead. The father simply shouted over and over, Emily!

"Where's Emily," I said, the father temporarily gaining control of my mouth.

"Ahriman brought her back too, baby," She said with a smile. "She's with him right now. W...We didn't know how you would react..." she trailed off.

"So basically, she's a hostage, and you're just the ransom note," I said, the monster hunter reasserting dominance.

"Don't be that way, baby" Sam pleaded. "He just wants his property back; then things will be just like they were."

"They'll never be like they were Sam." I interrupted. "You're dead. Emily is dead, and I bet the bastard you're trying to canonize, is the one who sent the monsters that killed you." I said, the volume of my voice growing as the reality of the situation and the pain in my heart grew. Samantha's face grew still, then angry as I continued. "You don't even have your own will; you're controlled by that bastard."

Her face transformed then. It took on a haughty, sinister demeanor. "Give me the amulet, you pathetic human." Her voice was that of someone else. Whatever part of my wife that remained in her body was shoved aside and a rasping male voice was issuing the commands.

"Fuck you," I said. The barrel of my pistol, that had been sagging slowly towards the ground rose once more to center between my dead wife's breasts.

"You'll get the amulet over my dead body." In retrospect, that may not have been the best choice of words.

Sam's eyes turned blood red, and her fangs popped down with an audible click. "As you wish." Came the harsh reply as the creature that used to be my wife lunged.

God help me, I hesitated. It was a fraction of a second, but it was long enough. Before I could refocus, she was on me. A sweeping hand knocked my .45 to the side a split second before her body crashed into mine and sent us both to the floor.

I was toast. I knew it beyond a shadow of a doubt. No human has the strength to resist a vampire in unarmed combat. It's like wrestling a silverback gorilla on steroids. A hand like steel clamped down on my throat . Her other hand was casually pinning my gun hand to the floor. It may as well have been super glued there for all the movement I could achieve from it.

"Stupid human, no mortal can stand against me." She hissed with venom. "I'm going to bring you back as a zombie, so you can watch me torture and use your wife and daughter for all eternity." Samantha's fanged mouth started down to rip out my throat, and there wasn't a damned thing I could do about it.

There came a huge crash from my bedroom window and suddenly the weight of the vampire on my chest was removed. The hand that had been clenching my throat was torn away, leaving deep scratches from my throat and down my chest. I lay, half-stunned on the floor trying to make sense of what I was seeing.

The first thing I saw a pair of shapely female legs, snugly encased in what appeared to be black leather, standing between me and the crumpled form of my wife, lying against the far wall of my bedroom. There was a dent in the drywall from her impact. My eyes continued traveling up the form in front of me to take in a black silk top. Flowing waves of auburn hair flowed over it down between my savior's shoulder blades. Siobhan.

The being wearing the Samantha suit hissed loudly as it regained its feet. "Do not seek to thwart me, vampire! All your kind are mine to control. Kneel before your master!"

Siobhan just smirked "Please, I've felt more compelled by prepubescent girls." she sneered. "I think you've lost your mojo."

Sam's face transformed into a cunning expression. "Perhaps." She said with a sinister smile. "But when my creature returns this to me." She said holding up my amulet triumphantly. "Everything will change."

My eyes grew wide, and my hand flew to my chest, scrambling desperately to feel the amulet that was no longer there. A sound that I'd been hearing for a while now intruded on my consciousness. The pounding on my bedroom door was getting louder and louder.

"The next time we meet you will all kneel before me." She cackled.

With a blurring fast move, she flew out of my bedroom window just as the reinforced door to the room, gave way.

Lori and Jake entered in a rush. Saiga shotguns, cleared the corners of the room before both the barrels of both guns locked onto Siobhan like the black eyes of death.

Siobhan held her hands out to the sides and froze. "Hold!" I had shouted before they had a chance to pull the trigger.

Both guns continued to point at Siobhan's ample chest, but they held their fire. "Sitrep!" Barked Lori as she eyed the ancient Irish vampire coldly over the barrel of her Saiga.

"Clear," I said. "Siobhan just saved my life. Stand down."

Lori and Jake took a step back and lowered their shotguns to ready positions. I noticed Lori was only wearing a pair of sleep shorts and a thin pink t-shirt as she stood there with the big black shotgun grasped confidently in her hands. She looked like a model from one of those "Stacked and Packed" calendars you see in some of the gun shops. It would have been hot if, you know, I didn't think of her as a sister.

Jake had his uniform pants still on but was bare from the waist up. His chiseled six pack and bulging pecs seemed to get Siobhan's attention as she stood there with a speculative expression on her face. A small, fanged feeling of jealousy started chewing on things in my core. "What the hell, Dale? Get your head back in the game." I chastised myself, realizing that I was trying to take my mind off what had just happened in my bedroom.

"What the hell, Dale?" Said Jake, echoing my thoughts. Looking at the busted out window, he asked, "What happened?"

I took a deep breath and let it out with a loud sigh. "That fucking necromancer, Ahriman is his name, by the way, sent me a visitor." I looked up and locked eyes with Lori. "It was Sam."

Lori's eyes grew wide with shock. "She's alive?" she asked, her expression becoming puzzled.

"No," I said glumly. "She still came to visit, though."

Lori's expression became sad and sympathetic. The worst fear any hunter had was that someone he loved would be turned. It was a deeper fear than being turned yourself. Just imagine cutting off your mother's head as she tried to rip out your throat and you'll get some idea of just how deep that fear runs.

Jake cleared his throat. "Are you okay boss?" He asked gesturing at the claw marks, starting to ooze blood down my chest.

My hand came up once more in a vain effort to feel my amulet. "I'm fine, but Sam got away with my medallion. She'd have taken more than that if Siobhan hadn't shown up when she did." I looked at Siobhan quizzically. "Why did you show up when you did?" I asked.

"I was tracking the new vampire I told you about. Guess where it led?" she said sardonically.

I dropped down to a sit on my bed as I pondered the situation. Finally, I looked back up at Siobhan. "You said this creation was different somehow, right? Like the vamp had been created from another undead?"

Siobhan nodded in agreement. "That's how it felt."

"That son of a bitch must have turned them when they first died and had been keeping them in reserve this whole time." I gritted out through clenched teeth. "Why now?" I asked plaintively.

"We keep kicking his ass." Spoke up Jake. "He can't take us going head on, so he tried sneaking in the back door."

"That makes sense," I said, my head starting to nod in agreement. "We need to start trying to anticipate his next move now. After all, he got what he came for." I said as my hand trailed once more to the scratches on my neck and chest.

The room lapsed into silence as we all considered the implications of what had happened. Finally, I looked up and shook my head to clear it. "Well, we aren't going to solve that one tonight," I said looking back up at Lori and Jake. "You two should try to get what rest you can. We may have some long nights ahead of us."

"We can stay boss." Said Lori, glancing sidelong at Siobhan.

"It's alright," I said, nodding towards my beaten up bedroom door. "Get some sleep."

Nodding, they headed out.

Siobhan sat down next to me on the bed but didn't try to touch me. "I can't imagine what you must be feeling right now." She said. "It must have taken immense strength to resist giving her whatever she wanted."

I sat there for a moment, going back to the encounter in my mind. "I...It was at first, but I realized that it wasn't really her. She's just a monster now. A puppet used to try to get to me."

Siobhan sat for a moment, a troubled expression on her face. "Is that how you see us, Dale? As just monsters?" Her voice quivered as she said it. I could almost swear that moisture gathered in the corner of those glorious emerald eyes.

"I said, *she* was the monster. Not all of you." I tentatively reached over and took her cool hand in mine. "My wife is gone. That part that made her what she was, no longer exists."

Siobhan sniffed miserably, keeping her eyes downcast to where our hands held each other. Reaching out, I gently touched her chin and brought her head up so I could look her in the eye. "I never knew the Siobhan that was human. The vampire is all I've ever known, so our relationship has suffered no loss."

"So you see me as more than just a monster?" She asked, her bottom lip trembling slightly.

Heaven help me. How could a centuries old master vampire look so vulnerable all of the sudden? The cynical part of me suggested that it was all just manipulation. "But to what end?" speculated the other side of me that appreciated the beautiful creature in front of me. "She has nothing to gain by it."

I refocused my attention back and said, "When I looked at my wife at the end, when Ahriman took control, all I could see was the tool, the puppet used to acquire what he desired. When I look at you, I see a person with no strings making her dance to another's tune. I just see you." I said.

She smiled tremulously then. "Thank you, Dale. I feared you seeing your wife as a vampire had done irrevocable harm."

"Naw," I said with a grin. "Us tough guys know how to keep things in perspective." I looked at her questioningly then. "Do you sense any change in how you feel about me, though?" I asked. "After all, my undead controlling mojo just got taken away from me."

Siobhan's head cocked to the side in thought. "No," She said speculatively. "My feelings haven't changed at all. But then again, I still feel a great deal of power inside you still."

"So is it just the power that's attracting you?" I said. It was my turn to feel vulnerable for some reason.

Siobhan leaned in and placed a soft kiss on my lips. "There is much more to you than the power from some musty old amulet, Dale Frost."

Siobhan offered to spend the rest of the night with me of course, but once again I begged off. After the events of the previous few hours, I needed time to myself. As dawn started to lighten the eastern horizon, I finally got up and trudged into the kitchen, searching for coffee.

Lori was seated at the kitchen table with a steaming cup in her hand. I moved gratefully to the coffee, getting my own cup of inspiration. "Glad you have some pants on this time," I said with a grin. "Highly unprofessional, fighting the forces of evil in your underwear. You know that, right?"

Lori snorted derisively. "Fine, I'll take the time to get fully dressed before I come to save your ass the next time. Besides, you're the only guy who complains when I come into a room with my pants off." She said with a wink.

It was my turn to snort. "I bet they'd be scared to death if you barged in wearing no pants and packing that shotgun like you did last night. That was some scary shit."

"You'd be surprised how certain guys would react to a naked girl packing a big gun." She said with a knowing smile.

"Eww, now I need brain floss to get the image out of my head. I said with a dramatic shudder.

Both of us smiling slightly, we sat in companionable silence and nursed our coffee.

"I noticed Siobhan didn't stay the night." She said after a while.

"Sleeping with Siobhan after fighting off my dead wife just seemed wrong somehow," I replied.

"What about Emily?" said Lori softly. "Did he bring her back too?"

I stared aimlessly into my coffee cup for a moment. "That's what Sam said." I managed to get out after a minute, with only a slight crack in my voice.

Lori reached out and gave my hand a squeeze. "I'm sorry Dale." She said, with her heart in her eyes. "You know it's not really them anymore, though, right?"

"I know." I sighed "But I can't stand the thought of even a part of them being in that bastards clutches. They deserve to rest in peace." I said.

Lori reached up and used her thumb to wipe a tear that had been running down my cheek, unnoticed. "We'll get the bastard." She said strongly. "We'll put him back in a hole and your family will get the rest they deserve."

8

Ahriman smiled triumphantly as his creature entered the room. Finally, after all, these eons the power would be his. It would take but a little spell work to finish the enchantments. Then, the full power of the amulet would come to bear.

Samantha approached her master demurely. "Your amulet, Master." She said holding the piece of gold on it's broken chain out to him.

He snatched the amulet out of her hand and clutched it tightly to him as if he thought she would try to keep it for her own. "Yesssss" He hissed as the power infused him. He felt himself growing stronger and stronger. Soon he would achieve his strength of old and then finish the enchantment so as to become the god of the undead in truth!

The smile that had been spreading across his face stopped, quickly becoming a frown as the power transfer from the amulet suddenly guttered and dropped to a trickle. He opened his hand and stared in consternation as the last of its power drained into him. He continued to stare at it in disbelief. The power was barely half of what he had anticipated. What had gone wrong?

Slowly, a burning anger kindled itself in his chest as he considered the diminished amulet. Just as the amulet fed power into him, so it must also have fed power into the worthless human hunter. "How could this be?" He questioned silently, pondering the enchantments that he had laid on the amulet, so long ago. He started pacing in agitation as the answer grew in his mind. He didn't get the chance to complete the enchantment. It must have left an opening of sorts. An opening through which some of the amulet's power had leaked as it sat on the bare skin of the man's chest, directly over his heart.

"Nooooo!" He shouted, shaking clenched fists in rage at the heavens. All this time and planning, for nothing!

"Master, what's wrong?" Came the timid voice of the human's dead wife.

An irrational spurt of rage coursed through him, directed at the cowering form in front of him. One of the fists that had been clenched in hate at the heavens came slashing down, knocking the creature across the room to slam into the far wall.

As quickly as the rage had come, it was gone again. He considered what he knew as he resumed pacing. "It might be possible," he muttered to himself. Yes, it might just be possible to retrieve that which had been leached out. It would require the sacrifice of the human, but that was of no consequence. He intended all along to end the man's miserable existence. After all, people needed to learn what happened to them when they attempted to thwart his will. It was quite possible in fact that the sacrifice could also generate the power he needed to complete the enchantments on his amulet at the same time.

A gloating smile crossed his lips as he contemplated a future. A future where he tore the still beating heart out of the insolent human's chest and thereby cemented permanent control of all undead to his will.

++++

Money and John were sitting up in their respective beds when we got into the office, later that morning. "How are you guys feeling?" I asked as we entered the room.

"Weak as a newborn chick." Grumbled John.

"Yeah" piped in Money. "Feels like my heads packed with cotton or something. Like my brain's running at half speed."

I shook my head and tried to look consoling. "Wights are a nasty business, but at least you can recover from their whammy. Mummys now, you don't come back from mummy rot unless you've got a powerful cleric with you." I finished with a shudder.

"I'll take your word for it," John said glumly. "It's like I can't call up half of what I used to know."

I nodded in acknowledgment. "All part of the whammy. We'll get you back up to top speed in no time. Just you wait and see."

We chatted idly for a short time before Lori, Jake and I headed off in our separate directions.

I spent the morning filling out government paperwork for the wights we'd, well okay I, had taken down. There was a hefty price on the heads of those things. $150,000 a pop to be exact. It didn't seem like enough, given that two of my people could barely walk right now, but at least it was a start.

About three o'clock I was just starting to think I needed to go down to the gun range and burn off some frustrations when my cell phone rang. Looking at it, I saw Alex's name on the screen. "Hey Alex, what've you got?" I asked.

"What, I can't just call to say hi? Maybe see how you're doing?" He said in a mock injured tone.

"Cut the crap," I responded jovially. "You never call just to see how I'm doing. That would be against the unwritten guy code, after all."

Alex chuckled a little. "Okay, okay, you got me there." he conceded. "Anyway, I think I might have picked up something from the unexplained death files."

"Oh really?" I said, sitting up in my chair.

"Yup," he said. "There's been an uptick in strange deaths down in the south side."

I snorted a bit. "What's strange about that?" I asked in a derisive tone. "There's death down there all the time."

"True," he said seriously. "But these bodies have been showing up *without* the bullet holes or knife wounds.

"That is strange," I remarked. "Do they have anything in common?

"Not really." He replied. "They seem to be mostly street people, homeless, prostitutes, etc., but there doesn't seem to be any commonality along age, race or gender lines. They're just showing up dead with no obvious cause noted."

I thought about that for a moment before responding. "Still, that isn't all that unusual for that area," I said, playing devil's advocate.

"Yeah I know, but there was one report that has me looking in that direction." He replied. "It seems a group of guys was walking home from a bar down there when they noticed what looked to be a man hunched over something lying on the ground. One of the guys shouted out, asking what the guy was doing. Here's the funny part. All the guys in the group swear that when this dude looked up from what turned out to be a body, his eyes were glowing this weird green color. Have you heard of anything like that before?"

"That's a new one on me," I said, shaking my head. "But there's a lot about this case that doesn't make sense." I went on to describe the events of the previous evening.

"Fuck man, are you alright?" Asked Alex, the concern evident in his tone.

"I'll live I suspect" I replied somberly. Can you get a read on where the killer, if there really is one, is based?" You know, triangulate based on where the bodies were found, or something?

Alex snorted. "This isn't an episode of CSI, dude. Shit like that doesn't often work in the real world." He replied. "Still, most of the deaths seem to occur within about a twenty block square."

I sighed at that. Given the size of Chicago's city blocks, that was a lot of ground to find one guy in. "Any mortuaries or cemeteries in the area?" I asked on impulse.

"Several at a guess," Alex replied. "You want me to put a list together?"

"Yeah," I replied. "It's a bit obvious, but it gives us a place to start."

"Alright man, I'll look into it further. Hey, you be careful." He said in concern. "You never know when this guy might decide to come after you again."

"Why bother?" I asked a little gruffly. "The son of a bitch already has what he was after. It's my turn to go after him for once."

"Still, watch your six. Nobody ever accused necromancers of being rational." He said before hanging up.

At sundown, I gave Siobhan a call.

"Hello love," she said with just a hint of Irish burr. Things inside me fluttered a bit at her greeting. Partly because I still wasn't sure that a hunter having a relationship with a vampire was kosher, partly because I was touched by the term of endearment.

"Hey, Siobhan," I replied. "Any news on...the new vampire or this Ahriman guy?" I just couldn't bring myself to say "my wife" especially given who I was talking to.

"I was able to track her for quite some time before the sense of her, simply vanished." Said Siobhan in a troubled tone. "I think her master may be able to shield her, and himself, from detection."

"Which way was she headed?" I asked.

"South and a little east." She replied. "I was still quite a distance from her when I lost the track."

I nodded at that. "Alex said there'd been some unexplained deaths in the south side recently. Over and above what's usual for that area. He thinks there might be a connection."

"I will send some of my people into the area to investigate. Perhaps we can get some indication of where the necromancer is that the human police might miss." She replied.

"Are you sure that's a good idea?" I asked in a troubled tone. "This guy can control undead after all."

"I understand your concern, but that very sense of compulsion may very well allow us to pinpoint his location." She replied seriously.

"Tell your people to be careful just the same. The last thing I want to do is put down one of yours because they were compelled to attack." I replied.

"You be careful as well love." She said seriously. "He may have his amulet back, but he still might carry a grudge."

"I doubt he'll give me a second thought now that he has what he wants," I said dismissively.

"All the same, be careful. You still have some power over the undead yourself. He may see that as a threat." She said in a slightly scolding tone.

"I'll be careful," I promised. "Let me know if you find out anything."

"I'll keep in touch," she said in a sultry tone that gave a different twist to the word touch than the sentence implied. I clicked off before I was tempted to explore the various meanings of the word.

I sat there for awhile. Things had been going so fast that I hadn't really considered the fact that in all actuality, I was a necromancer myself. Had I always been one? Some genetic mutation or something? Or was the power simply borrowed from the amulet? Would it remain with me or would it leech away now that the amulet was gone?

I closed my eyes and searched within myself. I've never been one for meditation or that kind of thing, so it was hard. All the sounds that I didn't hear as I went about my day seemed to come suddenly to the fore. The buzzing of the fluorescent lights, the low sound of traffic on the surrounding streets, things that are just white noise today seemed to all be conspiring to break my concentration.

Slowly, I was able to focus my concentration inward. At first, there was nothing, but random thoughts. Things like "This is stupid. You aren't some monk on a mountain top, dumbass." You know things like that.

Eventually, I got past that and started to sense something different. There seemed to be a black globe of...something, power?, at the center of my being. As my focus narrowed to that spot, I started to sense ephemeral black tentacles of the substance undulating from the globe, connecting to things I couldn't see with my eyes.

I chose a single tentacle at random and tried to reach out and get a sense of where it led. Abruptly,

I just knew that there was a vampire on the roof of a building across the street. The...flavor, for lack of a better term, was familiar. It was one of Siobhan's people. She was still watching over me like a mother hen. I didn't know if I should be flattered or annoyed.

Thinking about Siobhan, I withdrew back to my orb of power. I like the sound of that. "Orb of Power!" Anyway, I went back and focused on the tentacles emanating from it. One, in particular, seemed to draw my attention. Concentrating on it, I got the sense of Siobhan once more. It was stronger and more direct. I knew without thinking where this tentacle would lead. On impulse, I followed it.

The tentacle ended in another globe. I sensed that it was larger than my own, but not by much. It seemed to call to me. I drew ever closer until my awareness...made contact.

She knew I was there immediately. There seemed to be an almost instinctive defensive reaction trying to push me away from her core, but just as quickly as it started, it stopped. A sense of recognition came through the link we shared, followed quickly by a sense of welcome and love.

My god! She really did love me. A large part of me always suspected her of indulging in some manipulative con game designed to increase her own power. After all, my experience with vampires told me that power was more seductive to them than blood.

A sense of acknowledgment came to me then, as if she could read my mind. It was more than that, however. It was true communion. I was so new to this; I had no walls in place to defend myself, and her...she dropped her walls and let me in.

Our power mixed. I instantly knew her better than anyone I had ever known before. Even Sam, before she died. Siobhan's whole life was laid out before me. I knew all her dreams and fears. I watched her life through the centuries; I saw the good and evil she had wrought and the turning points in her life that had made her what she was today.

The sharing went both ways. She knew all that I was, my strengths and the weaknesses that I hid away from everyone. The petty and disgusting things that all humans have hidden in the dark corners of their souls were there for her perusal. She accepted them without qualification. As that realization struck, I knew that I had no problem accepting who she was either. Yes, there was a darkness in her, a potential to the evil that she fought every single day. Her motives were not altogether altruistic in that regard. She controlled the evil because she knew that was the path to longer life and more power.

I found I could get behind those notions. Not so much the power for power's sake but power enough to protect me and those around me from any foe, no matter how strong. I sensed her agreement of that and the notion of how powerful we could become together.

All the while we were communing, I could sense the connection between us growing. As if exercising a long unused muscle was making it stronger and more capable.

"You astound me, my love." I actually heard her words in my mind, over our connection. "I never expected you to immerse yourself so deeply in your power."

"It's there inside of me. I just set about trying to explore it." I replied across the miles separating us.

"You should be proud. Most undead never reach this level of communication or power." She said in quiet awe.

"I'm not undead, though. I...I'm a necromancer, I guess." I said, still troubled by the apparent fact.

"You are what your life and circumstances made you." She said, the feeling of acceptance and love, once more flooding through our link. "You need not put a name to it or feel bad about it. I, above all others, see who you are, and above all else, you are still a good man.

I did my best to return the feelings of acceptance and, god help me, the love that I felt towards her. As intimately as we had shared, there could be nothing less. I felt quiet joy come from her then, as I finally accepted what she'd known for a while now.

I was never one to believe in destiny. I always figured we were put on this earth to make our own way and maybe learn a thing or two before we passed on. But this, this had the feel of a long-missing puzzle piece falling into place, creating a picture of profound beauty and depth.

As I sat there at my desk in communion with my soul's mate, a dark presence started to intrude. A feeling of power was coming closer to me in the physical world. "Siobhan, what is that?" I asked, hoping her greater experience would give me a clue.

"I...I don't know," her voice once more came over our bond. "I think...."

All of the sudden an immense wave of power overwhelmed my mind, blocking out all sensation. As I floated in a sea of blackness, a new voice came to me. *"STUPID HUMAN! DID YOU THINK YOU COULD USE THE POWER YOU STOLE FROM ME WITHOUT MY KNOWLEDGE?*

The pain of the words tore at my soul. Pain so great I could barely think. Instinctively, I tried to erect a barrier against the jagged power, pushing hot needles into my psyche. I was on the razor's edge of insanity at that point, staring into an abyss from which there was no recovery. As I teetered on edge, I was bolstered suddenly by a new presence. Power coursed through my bond to Siobhan, creating a bubble of some kind that surrounded my fracturing mind. It was fragile and tenuous, but it was holding.

As the pressure of Ahriman's will was pushed back, I realized she was using every ounce of power at her disposal to protect me. It gave me enough space to gather my wits into something approaching coherence and add my own power to the shield she had cast around me.

The synergy we had created with our bond translated into power over and above what we could achieve alone. The shield got thicker and harder. Once it was stable, we started pushing back.

The fight was brutal. Ahriman had the wisdom of ages and huge power at his beck and call. He used them ruthlessly. He was outnumbered, however. The combined power of Siobhan and I were sufficient, just barely, to push him completely from my mind.

A final thought penetrated like a spear before he was cast out completely. *"Come to me, mortal or your wife and child will suffer for all eternity*!" A vision came on the heels of his words then. He was standing in the parking garage of my own building, clutching the hand of a beautiful redheaded girl. Her eyes seemed to lock on my presence, and she wailed. *"**DADDY! HELP ME!**"*

My eyes snapped open. My feet carried me to my office door even before my vision came back into focus. Almost blindly I sprinted down the hallway and through the reception area to the elevator. I thought I heard someone shout as the steel doors closed behind me. My brain didn't acknowledge the words. All I could think about was my little girl in the hands of a monster, her cry for help ringing again and again in my brain, drowning out anything else

The .45 appeared in my hand, seemingly of its own volition as I stepped out into the parking garage. There was no one there. Pistol at the ready I scanned the visible areas of the parking garage, looking for Emily.

As my breathing stabilized, my brain once more engaged. The sense of Siobhan asserted itself. A feeling of calmness infused me, allowing me to think. "Go cautiously love. You know this is a trap. I'll be by your side shortly."

I took the words to heart and sent a feeling of acknowledgment back along our bond, tempered with a warning. She knew I worried that Ahriman could control her. I started down the driveway between the sparsely occupied parking spots. Not many people were here after dark. A movement to my left had me spinning that direction. The tritium spot on the front sight of my pistol settled in the center of Ahriman's chest. He was alone.

"Where's my daughter, you bastard." I ground out between clenched teeth.

A dusty chuckle came from Ahriman. He looked like just another guy I realized as I studied him over my sights. Shorter than me by quite a bit, maybe 5' 5" or 5' 6". He was thin in a way that suggested whipcord strength not malnutrition. Black hair framed Mediterranean features and skin tone. He was dressed in a white button-down shirt with slacks and a blazer. Perfect for blending into the heavy business area that surrounded us. The most remarkable features about him were his eyes. The were black, like the twin openings of a double-barreled shotgun, cold but ready to wreak instant havoc. "The girl is safe...for now," he said in the classic movie bad guy response to that question.

"Okay, Ariman," I said, keeping the gun at the ready, but relaxing my stance a little. "You already have the medallion. What more could you possibly want with me?"

"Simple enough." He responded with a shrug of his narrow shoulders. "You have stolen some of the power from the amulet. I want it back." He said, his voice going hard at the end.

"Oh, is that all?" I said as I began pretending to check my pockets with my free hand. "I know I have it around here somewhere," I said in an absent-minded tone.

"***DO NOT TRIFLE WITH ME HUMAN!***" He shouted in a voice that seemed too loud for his small body to have made.

I took an involuntary step back. One of these days, my inner smart ass was going to get me killed. A sense of sardonic agreement came floating over my link to Siobhan.

Ahriman quickly calmed himself and continued. "You will come to me as a willing sacrifice. If you do, I will release your wife and daughter. You will all be together in peace, in the afterlife."

I heard the ding of the elevator as I opened my mouth to tell the bastard where he could stick his offer. The doors opened, and my Dreadnoughts streamed out, shotguns pointed at Ahriman as they took up defensive positions around me.

Ahriman seemed unconcerned. "Well," he said. "What's it to be? Will you come with me now or suffer the knowledge that your wife and child will be forever tormented in my possession?"

"I think I'll take door number three, Bob," I said in my best game show contestant voice. I put my gun in its holster and raised my hands to my head. "Dreadnoughts, light this fucker up." I ground out to my team as my fingers went into my unprotected ears.

Five fully automatic Saiga 12 gauge shotguns spat fury at Ahriman. Gunsmoke and concrete dust from the wall behind Ahriman's position obscured my vision, and the necromancer disappeared in the haze.

A bare few seconds later the shotguns clicked on empty magazines, and I drew my .45 once more as my team placed fresh ones home. Spreading out, we approached Ahriman's position. The '90's Corolla he'd been standing behind seemed a little worse for wear. Sweeping in to get a view in front of the car, we found...nothing. No body, no blood, nothing.

"It was a projection; he was never really here." Said a familiar female voice behind us.

We whipped around to see Siobhan standing by the street entrance to the parking garage. With a flash of brilliance, I proclaimed, "Uh, what?"

"It was a projection." She reiterated. "He used magic to project an illusion of himself. He was never really here." She concluded.

"He sure as hell looked real" Said Jake, with a growl.

"Tis ancient magic the creature possesses. A sorcerer from ages past on top of his necromancy." She replied, her Irish accent stronger than usual.

"Crap," I said. "How do we fight something like that?"

"Ye have power and weapons of your own, to be sure. I myself am no slouch in that regard." She said with a smile as she approached.

Being this close together, the link between us was almost palpable in its strength. Siobhan flowed into my arms. It felt right, like a key sliding into a lock. It was so natural seeming that I didn't think anything of it until the tittering started.

I could feel my face heating up as I turned to glare at my crew. They all stood there grinning with knowing expressions on their faces. Jerks.

"What are you guys, twelve?" I asked with temerity. "This isn't middle school, for crying out loud."

The Dreadnoughts tried, without much success, to regain their composure. For her part, Siobhan just snuggled in closer and laid the side of her head against my chest.

Lori was the first one to recover some semblance of composure. "What now boss?" she asked. "He still has Sam and Emily, even if they're just a shade of what they once were."

Reluctantly I released my hold on Siobhan and turned to face my guys. "We've got to find the bastard before we can do anything." I said somberly "Alex and some of Siobhan's people are out looking. We think he might be holed up somewhere on the south side of town."

The crew groaned at the thought. "Well there's good and bad neighborhoods both down there, maybe we'll get lucky." Said Ray.

"Alex is trying to map out the likely areas to concentrate on. Hopefully, we'll have some idea of where to search tomorrow." I replied. "For now, go home and get some rest. We'll hit it fresh in the morning."

Everyone except Lori and Jake grumbled their ascent and turned back towards the elevator. Those two stood ready to resume their guard duty from the previous evening. "You guys too," I said with a nod towards the elevator. "I'll stick with Siobhan. We have some things to go over anyway."

"I'll just bet you do." Said Jake with a crooked grin and raised eyebrows. I started to growl at him, but Lori turned and punched him in the shoulder.

"Ow!" He said, grabbing his shoulder. "What was that for?"

Lori just gave him an arched look as she turned for the elevator. "Come on, you big adolescent. I'll buy the first round at Smitty's." Having said that, they both turned with a wave and headed for the elevator.

I turned back to Siobhan, my arms going back around her of their own volition. I looked into her emerald gaze and summoned all of the eloquence at my disposal. "Hi," I said.

She smiled up at me. "Hi, yourself."

I could have stayed in her embrace forever, but the real world was intruding on my peace of mind.

"What now?" I said. "Is Ahriman going to be able to penetrate my mind and screw with me whenever he wants? I asked.

"Siobhan's eyes became serious. "He's powerful, there can be no doubt of that, but I can teach you to shield yourself well enough to protect your mind. Indeed, the power you contributed to our combined defenses should give you some idea of how to create such a warding on your own."

I thought back and realized that she was probably right. "It took both of us to ward him off, though. And he still got through with his parting shot about Emily." I said with concern.

"Aye, that he did, but the shield we built was off the cuff and unplanned. With deliberation and concentration, it can be made much stronger." She said in a comforting tone.

"Cool," I said in reply. "Is there anyway we can use this power to find the rat bastard?" I asked, a steel edge of anger lacing my tone.

She looked at me quizzically before replying. "I have been unsuccessful in my own efforts in that regard." She said, frustration evident on her beautiful features. "Perhaps you can do better. Your power does seem a bit different. Tell me, how were you able to find me last night when we bonded?" She cast her eyes down demurely on the last word.

I went over how I had discovered the orb of power at my core and how I could follow the tentacles emanating from it to find various undead. "Speaking of which," I said with a mock scowl. "Is it really necessary to have your people spying on me from the next building over?"

"Hell yes," she said strongly. "I protect that which I value, and you have an uncanny ability for finding trouble."

"I also have a lot of really tough boys and girls with guns around me. That tends to tilt the scales in my favor generally." I said, smiling crookedly at her.

"Better safe than sorry love," she said with a warm smile. "Now" she continued, getting back to business. "Do one of these tentacles you told me about by chance lead to the one we're looking for?"

I stared at her stupidly for a moment. "Honestly, that hadn't occurred to me. Once we connected last night, I kind of lost track of things for awhile." I said, with what was undoubtedly, a stupid grin on my face.

"Aye, it was a bit distractin' at that." She replied with a grin of her own. "Still, you should try again. It may leave you open to attack, but I'll be here to slam the shields home should the monster try to gain entry to your thoughts once more."

"It was hard getting to that point last night," I said in concern. "It took a lot of meditation and focus to find that spot."

"The first time is always hardest. That you were able to accomplish it at all without instruction, especially your first time trying, is a remarkable feat." She said with a little wonder in her voice. "Still, there are better places to attempt the task than a parking garage."

"What do you have in mind?" I asked

"Well, your place was a bit drafty after my dramatic entrance into your bedroom last night. It is also a place known to our adversary. I think you should come to my place tonight. Just for safety's sake, mind." She said with an innocent smile on her face.

It wasn't in me to resist her anymore. I really didn't even want to try. There was one thing that gave me some reluctance, however. "Um, I don't want to seem rude, but is it wise to surround ourselves with undead when our adversary, as you put it, can control them?" I asked, wincing slightly and waiting for the angry retort.

Anger wasn't forthcoming, however. "A fair point." She said consideringly. "We really don't know what the fiend is capable of." She paused for a minute in thought. "Still, I have more than one property available to me and not all of them are filled with my kin."

It was Siobhan's first time in my mustang. She actually purred in delight as she sat down on the buttery soft, black leather seats and the throaty growl of the engine sent its challenge to all comers. "I don't know if I approve." She said with a mock frown. "A beast like this will be turning all the girl's heads."

I looked over at her, my eyes taking in the black leather pants and the ruffled button down silk blouse that seemed to be her preferred fighting attire. Not all the buttons on the blouse were buttoned either, leaving plenty of creamy white skin showing to excellent advantage. "Pot calling the kettle black there darlin," I said, leering cheerfully at her. Her sultry chuckle echoed through the night as the Mustang's liquid black paint job reflected the shadows and streetlights. Turning left out of the parking garage, we eased down the late night streets of Chicago.

9

Following Siobhan's directions, I soon found myself pulling into parking structure of a high-rise apartment building. The express elevator took us straight to the penthouse. I guess I shouldn't have expected anything less from the Master of Chicago.

Siobhan's place was not what I expected. Being a high-rise penthouse, I was expecting chrome and black leather, maybe furniture that took an instruction manual just to sit on. Nothing could be further from the truth. The place was done up in earth tones, tans and browns for the most part. The furniture, though no doubt high end, was built for comfort. The couch I settled myself on at Siobhan's gesture had brown leather so soft, it made the seats of the Mustang seem like a rough country cousin in comparison. As I settled my weight on it, I was enfolded in welcoming luxury. The tension in my muscles that I hadn't consciously known about, immediately started to ease. I let out a grateful sigh.

Siobhan curled up beside me as I took in the living room. "This is nice," I said, turning my attention back to her. "It's more comfortable and homey than I would expect from a penthouse."

"Aye," she said, resting her head on my shoulder. "I keep it such, to remind me of my roots and the feelings of home."

She looked up and met my gaze. I lost myself in her emerald eyes for a moment before leaning towards her. She met me halfway, and our lips touched. It was a soft, languorous kiss. A thing of sharing and comfort. Her lips, while cool, were not disturbingly so. I closed my eyes and savored the sensation. The arm that had been resting on the back of the couch came around and drew her to me in a warm embrace as the kiss deepened into something more passionate.

The opposite arm came across, and I settled my hand on the soft blouse covering her ribcage. As our tongues met with increasing passion, my hand rose up her ribs and my thumb lightly, grazing the side of her breast. She shuddered slightly, and a sigh escaped her. Her delicate hand, that concealed incredible power rose to lightly stroke my cheek, before sliding down to rest against my chest.

She pulled back from our kiss and looked into my eyes once more. "I've waited too long for this night." She said the urgent need in her eyes reflected my own. "I'll not wait a moment longer."

I remained speechless as she uncoiled from the couch and stood before me. The bond between us was a vibrant thing, pulsing with the desire we both felt. She reached out and offered me her hand. I took it as I flowed to my feet and she led me down a short hallway to a richly appointed oak door. The latch made a soft click as it closed behind us.

I've never laid on silk sheets. They felt incredible and weren't near as slippery as I would have thought. Their softness paled in comparison to the alabaster skin of the woman who was curled up contentedly at my side; one leg was thrown over my thighs. "Well now, that was worth the wait." She said in a warm fuzzy tone.

"That it was," I said as I curled the arm that lay beneath her and drawing her closer to me. The bond between us opened wide as our passion had increased. It gave us insights into each other's wants and needs so that we moved together in near perfect unity. Instead of a clumsy first time coupling, we'd made magic. Okay, I know that sounds corny, but whatever...shut up.

We laid there awhile longer before Siobhan disentangled herself from our embrace and stood beside the bed. My breath caught as my gaze traveled up her form. Statuesque legs led up to curvaceous hips and a narrow waist The flawless alabaster skin of her taut abdomen and torso, accentuated perfectly formed breasts with light pink areolas.

Emerald green eyes twinkled down at me from behind tousled auburn locks. A sultry smile spread across her lips as she caught me staring. "Not bad for four hundred thirty seven don't you think?" She said, winking at me.

I pulled myself together and put on a considering expression. "That's for sure," I said with a leering smile. "I wouldn't put you past four hundred twenty-five, personally." That got me hit with a pillow...hard. "Sorry!" I said, laughing as I covered my head defensively. "Why don't you come back to bed and I'll show you what I really think," I said with a grin of my own.

Siobhan chuckled, but instead of rejoining me, she picked up a satin robe and put it on. Much to my disappointment. "Get up you wicked man." She said with a slight smile. "We've business to attend to before morning light intrudes."

My face became serious as I refocused on the problem at hand. "That we do," I said gruffly as I swung my legs over the side of the bed and reached for my pants. "We have too much life to enjoy to let some asshole keep getting in the way."

Nestled on the couch once more, Siobhan took my hand and stared into my eyes. "I want you to concentrate and go back to that place where your power lies."

I closed my eyes and sent my focus inward. It was easy this time. The sense of our bond led me right to it. My orb of power had grown. Probably because the tentacle that traveled off to Siobhan, had at least tripled in size to my perception. "Got it," I said, keeping my eyes closed in concentration.

"Good," said Siobhan softly. "Now, I want you to explore the tentacles. See if any call to you in particular or if there are any that feel...familiar."

Just because that's how I roll, the first tentacle I explored was hers. I sent a wave of lust down it. A cosmic goose to the posterior, if you will. Siobhan chuckled and told me to get my mind back on business. After a little practice, I began to get a sense of the creatures who connected with my power, without having to concentrate on individual tentacles. A whole new world opened to my senses.

I was surprised at the amount of undead there were in this town. Vampires, of course, hundreds of them. A few of them even approached Siobhan's level of power. I carefully avoided them. There were also other varieties. A lot of ghosts roamed

Chi-Town, as you might expect. They had the feel of residual energy about them. Like an after image imprinted on your retina when a flash goes off. There were also pockets of ghouls and zombies spread around the city. I could sense that they were quiescent at the moment. Held by outside forces. I think they were actually buried in the cemeteries around the city, warded against rising by whatever cleric had performed their burial rights.

I didn't ,however, feel the presence of Ahriman. There was no clue about where Sam or Emily might be either.

"I can't sense them," I said after awhile, frustration clearly present in my tone.

"Keep looking." Said Siobhan encouragingly. "Look for anything out of the ordinary, don't just focus on the individual creatures."

I tried to do as she instructed. I pulled my awareness back, trying to get an overview of the entire area while simultaneously overlaying a mental map of the area. I was immediately discouraged. Chicago and the surrounding suburbs constitute a huge area, and though they were more plentiful than I had originally guessed, there was just too few undead in the area to spot any patterns. There were vast blank spots on my mental map that were too large to investigate.

Sighing in frustration, I tried narrowing my focus once more. I zeroed in on the south side of town, looking for any anomalies in the area both Alex and Siobhan had kind of pointed to as a possible hiding spot.

The spots without undead activity were still large. There were several undead moving around the area. My internal sense told me that they were Siobhan's people, out searching, in her direction.

I continued to scan for what seemed like hours. As my brain became numb, I absently focused on one blip on my internal map. I watched idly as it moved along at a fairly steady pace with only small pauses.

Suddenly, it disappeared. My head snapped up, and I focused sharply on the area, thinking that I must have dozed off and simply lost track of the vampire. That wasn't the case, however. There just wasn't anything visible in that area all of the sudden.

"What do you see love?" Asked Siobhan, sensing my renewed alertness.

"I...just lost one of your people," I said in a confused tone. "He was there one minute and then just, gone."

As I explained this to Siobhan the blip on my internal radar, suddenly appeared once more a short way from where I had last seen him. "Wait, he's back again," I exclaimed. It was like he popped out of a hole, or came out from behind a wall."

I zeroed in on the blip and got a sense of him over the tenuous link to my power. It was definitely one of Siobhan's people.

"Can you communicate mentally with your people?" I asked Siobhan abruptly.

Siobhan shook her head slightly. "I can sense them around the city, but I can't contact them telepathically." A sardonic smile curved her lips. "We do have these handy little devices, however." She said, holding up a cell phone.

"Oh yeah, right," I said with a slight blush.

I focused on the sense of the vampire once more. "Give Jameson a call and tell him to stop," I commanded as I focused intently on his signal.

Siobhan scrolled through her contacts briefly before hitting the call button. "Jamie dear, be a darling and stop where you are for a bit." She said sweetly when her minion answered. "Just do it...now." she said after listening briefly, her tone becoming a bit cooler.

My sense of err...Jamie stopped and stood in place. "Okay have him walk back the way he just came" I said urgently

After Siobhan passed on the request, the blip of Jamie the Vampire, started to reverse his track. I waited as patiently as I could as he proceeded back. Just where he had appeared before, he abruptly disappeared from my view once again.

"He disappeared again. Tell him to keep going," I said as I continued to try to penetrate whatever was blocking my perception of him. I couldn't get any sense of him for another minute or so before he appeared as if by, well...magic, a little farther along.

"Stop," I said, my voice raised a little with urgency. "I've got him again. Find out his location for me." I said, turning once more to face Siobhan.

She listened briefly to her phone before looking up to meet my eyes. "He's on Marquette Road, near Peoria street, in Englewood." She said

"What's there," I asked.

"He's standing in front of a large building. He can't see any identifiers on it. It might be a school.

There's a fence all the way around it." She said, repeating what she'd heard.

"Well, something there is blocking my perception of him," I said firmly. Does he get any sense of power or compulsion from the area?"

I waited briefly as Siobhan talked to her man. "He doesn't feel anything at all." She said finally, shaking her head.

I thought about that for awhile. The vampire that had seen this guy at Smitty's reported being drawn to Ahriman, so why wasn't Jamie. "You said that Ahriman was a sorcerer as well as a Necromancer, could he have cast some kind of blocking spell that keeps anyone inside it from being perceived?" I asked finally.

"I'm not as familiar with the way of sorcerers as all that." She replied musingly. "However I would think some such spell would be within the realm of possibility."

"Well, it's something we need to check out at any rate," I said, nodding my head with conviction. "I'll get my boys and girls first thing in the morning, and we'll head on over."

"I cannot help you during the day." Said Siobhan in a troubled tone.

"I know," I said sympathetically. "During the day, my guys have the ability to escape the sun if things get too hairy."

"You may need my strength and the aid of my people" She continued persuasively. "You don't know what may be housed in that building."

"You're right, I don't know what's in that building, but I do know that there is a necromancer out there somewhere who can control undead," I said in a leading way, hoping she would get my reluctance.

Siobhan actually growled in frustration. "Aye I get your meaning, but it goes against my very nature to wait in the shadows while those I care about entering into danger."

I reached over and stroked her cheek gently with the back of my hand. "I understand, believe me, but I need to go in knowing that my people aren't going to suddenly turn on me against their will. Against any other enemy, I'd gladly have you by my side. You know that, right?"

Siobhan pressed her cheek into my hand briefly before nodding. "I understand, and I'll abide by your wishes in this...for now."

My eyebrows rose at the qualifier as she continued on.

"But know this." She said as her expression became fierce. "Ahriman is an even greater threat to my people than to your own, and I will only hold my hand for so long before acting."

I suddenly saw past the beautiful girl to the powerful being with centuries of battle under her belt. I remembered suddenly that those soft, gentle hands that had embraced me earlier could just as easily pull my arms and legs off if I became a threat.

The cold dose of reality coursed down my spine, causing me to sit up straight and look at her seriously. I understand what you're saying." I said, meeting her gaze.

"Be sure that you do, my love," she said in an iron hard tone. "Because my first duty is to my people, no matter how I may feel personally."

I nodded at her sternly. "You know I won't interfere with your duties. My boys and girls just happen to be the best tool for this particular job." I said, taking her hand. "We may need the help of you and your people in the end. If that's the case, I just hope Ahriman isn't as powerful as I fear."

Siobhan squeezed my hand gently as she looked into my eyes. I saw my own fear reflected in them.

10

First light saw me back at the office. I'd paged the team and was on the phone with Alex. "That's right, Marquette and Peoria. There seems to be something hinky going on there."

"Hinky?" he said derisively. "Care to be more specific?"

"I can't really tell you more than that. It's this mojo I've got in my head, telling me where to go. I just wanted to give you a heads up so some overeager cop doesn't shoot at us when we go in, loaded for bear...or zombies." I replied.

Alex snorted. "Cops try to stay out of that area; it's too damned dangerous. You're more likely to come up against the locals, and they might be better armed than you are."

"I hear ya," I said, chuckling in agreement. "At least you'll have some idea of what's going on when the shooting starts."

"I'll have STAC in the area for backup. Just in case." Said Alex, his tone becoming serious.

"Sounds good." I replied, "I'll let you know what we find."

I was already geared up, so I headed to the ready room to brief my people. They were all there except for Money and John, of course. I felt a pang in my heart at having to leave them behind. Given the earliness of the hour, the Dreadnoughts were sucking down coffee like it was nectar from the gods.

"Good morning, boys and girls!" I said, trying to sound chipper.

My salutation was met with general grumbling and comments like, "What's so good about it." We were not morning people, in general.

"Given who you were hanging out with last night when we left, I gotta wonder if you were just hanging out or letting it all hang out?" Tommy asked with a leering smile and wiggling eyebrows.

That got a weary chuckle from the room anyway. "None of your business, I growled, my face going slightly red.

"Come on, boss." Said Petey with a goofy grin on his face. "We want details."

"You want details? Okay. We're going down to Englewood and breaking into a large building in hopes of finding a bunch of undead and their necromancer leader." I said, with a scowl on my face.

The grins fell immediately from their faces on hearing my pronouncement.

"You found where this necro is holed up then?" Asked Lori with a surprised expression on her face. "That was fast."

"Siobhan helped me use some of my new mojo to help narrow it down." I replied, nodding "There's something supernatural going on in that building. It's like there's a shield around it that stops any magical senses from penetrating, so we get to go down and check it out the old fashioned way."

"Are you sure that's a good idea?" Said Lori in speculation. "We're two down and going into an unknown situation. That doesn't sound optimal to me."

"It's not," I said bluntly. "But we've worked short before and probably will again."

I looked around the room. The expressions varied from slight boredom to trepidation. "Look, guys; this Ahriman creep has my wife and daughter. Yeah, I know they're dead, but I can't stand the thought of them being some jerk's meat puppet." I sighed before continuing "Having said that, I'm making this voluntary. I won't force you to go. I can't guarantee that there'll be any bounties worth the trouble, so you may be doing it for free. It's up to you with no hard feelings if you bow out."

Ray sat up from his slouched position at one of the tables. "So let me make sure I've got all this. This necro of yours has summoned zombies to our favorite bar. He summoned wights to ambush us at the graveyard and he's using your dead wife and daughter as bait to get to you. Does that about cover it?" He asked seriously.

"He probably raised those baby vamps we've been playing with here lately too," I added in helpfully.

He stood up and looked around the room. "Okay, I'm in. This fucker has got to go down. Anyone want to back out?" He asked.

His question was met with a chorus of things like, "Oh, hell no." and, "This fucker's going down." amidst the clatter of chairs sliding back across the linoleum floor as the Dreadnoughts stood in support.

A profound gratitude swelled in my chest as the team stood to face me, fierce expressions lighting their faces. "Best. Team. Ever!" I said with shining eyes. "Let's go kill this fucker."

+++

We pulled up in front of the building as the sun rose fully over the buildings to the east. It looked like a school that was probably built back in the '70's, but there was no name on the front, and the marquis out front didn't hold any announcements. As described by Siobhan's minion, there was a wrought iron fence around it, shielding the grounds from casual trespassers. A walkway led up to the front entrance, but all the windows were dark.

Much to our relief, it was early enough that there were no people in evidence to watch us make entry. Figuring that any bad guys that might be inside already know we were there we lined up in our assault formation right at the front door.

With John down, we needed another big body to stand beside Petey on the front shields, so I took up a shield and moved into position. There was some grumbling about the stupidity of leading from the front, but it quickly quieted down.

To me, it made complete sense. Not only was I big enough to handle a shield efficiently, but I also had my undead control mojo to fall back on. Hopefully, that would make a difference.

I tested the door and found it locked as expected. Motioning behind me, I brought Ray up to pick the lock. No need to destroy property if we didn't need to. Lori and Ray moved then to grab one of the double doors each. On my signal, they pulled them rapidly open. Petey and I rushed in and took a knee, shields ready. Tommy and Jake were right behind us, Shotguns tracking over our heads, seeking targets.

The only thing that reached out to grab us was the smell. Decay and excrement with a chemical overtone assaulted our nostrils. "What the hell is that smell?" I muttered as we continued to scan the area.

"Smells like a meth den." Whispered Ray as he and Lori followed us through the doors. Being former Chicago PD, I guess he would know.

"That's all we need." I moaned quietly. "Tweaker zombies."

"Crap," said Tommy. "How will we know the living from the dead? Tweakers and zombies look pretty much the same."

"Tweakers will probably cower or try to run." Said Ray. "Zombies will be coming at us."

"Good point," I replied. "Try not to shoot any humans unless they try to shoot us first. Remember, drugs and guns go together like peas and carrots." I said in my best Forrest Gump impersonation. "Alright, let's move."

We were in a wide hallway with institutional, linoleum flooring. Dirt and graffiti covered the walls. Bits of trash and other things I didn't want to think about too long, littered the floor. We cleared each room as we came to it, prepared to be attacked by a horde of undead at any instant.

Nothing. The building remained quiet as a tomb. The further down the hall we went, the worse the tension and sense of foreboding became Finally, the hall ended at a T-junction with smaller hallways leading off to the left and right.

"Hold," I said quietly. "Let me try something." Closing my eyes briefly and accessed my mojo. To my shock, there were no tentacles to follow. I'd even lost my link to Siobhan. Part of me started to panic at that, but I took a couple of deep breaths and regained my composure.

Whatever spell that had been cast here must be more of a dampening field that stopped any detection within it, rather than a shield that protected those inside. At that thought, I started to feel trapped. What if it stopped me from turning undead as well? I hadn't had that ability for long enough to be dependant on it, but it sure was a nice backup.

"I can't get anything with my mojo." I said quietly "Whatever spell that's on this place is stopping me."

"Wonderful," muttered Tommy from behind me. "So, which way do we go?" he asked.

Falling back to plan B, I sniffed the air. "The smell seems stronger off to the left," I said, motioning that direction towards a pair of swinging doors at the end of the hallway. We eased down the hallway, the chemical smell becoming stronger and stronger as we went.

After clearing the one room on the hallway before reaching the double doors, we formed up to make entry. "On my mark. 3...2...1...GO." I said tersely.

Petey and I pushed through the doors, taking up our low positions behind the shields. The rest of the team followed in good order, and I heard the swinging doors close back into position in the silence that followed.

The only light in the large room, I'm guessing it was a gymnasium, was cast dimly by some grime encrusted skylights in the ceiling. The chemical smell overwhelmed all the others. I was kinda grateful for that.

The floor was littered with plastic containers and metal cans of varying sizes and shapes. In one corner, several tables were set up with various machines and containers. Hoses ran from one to the other. Other containers, apparently full, lined the walls to either side.

Oh yeah, the middle of the room was full of bodies. They were laying on the floor, scattered around the room haphazardly and unmoving. In the dim light, I couldn't tell if they were alive or dead, druggie or zombie.

As I took it all in, a voice came from the far corner of the room, opposite the equipment and hoses. "Ah, I see you've found my little hiding spot." Said Ahriman as he stepped into a small pool of light cast by an overhead skylight.

Our attention and weapons all focused on him as he stood there leering at us. "I would not advise firing your weapons in this room." He said with a feral grin. Things might become a bit...explosive if you do."

Crap, I'd fucked up. We've all heard stories of houses and hotel rooms exploding while people were cooking meth in them and I'd just led my guys right into the middle of one. "Put 'em down," I muttered as I slowly stood behind my shield to face Ahriman.

"Where are my wife and daughter?" I asked through gritted teeth, trying to maintain my composure.

"Obviously not here." Chuckled Ahriman, gesturing around the room. "As I said before, you must come to me in order to assure that your loved ones rest in peace. They are both quite beautiful. I will enjoy them both immensely if you do not do as I command." He said as his smile took on a greasy, leering quality.

I tamped down hard on my rage as well as the urge to pull my .45 and put two bullets in his brain pan. After the incident in the parking garage, I figured he wasn't really there anyway. "Where and when?" I ground out.

"Oakwoods Cemetery." He said promptly. "And just to make it dramatic, be there at midnight."

He started to fade out at that point, but just before he vanished completely he said, "Oh, and come alone, or you will never see your wife and child again."

After he had faded into invisibility, we stood there for a moment in silence. That's when I felt the spell that enfolded the building drop out of existence. Immediately, the forms on the floor began to stir. Crap.

With my mojo once more unsuppressed, I could feel the zombies hunger spark to life as they oriented on us. There were at least fifty of them in the room. "Back out people. We can't take all these guys with knives and axes.

The rest of the team moved back, followed by Petey and I as we kept our shields between us and the potential ravening horde. We were in a tight spot. If this many zombies got out among the general public, we could have a full blown zombie epidemic on our hands in no time.

By the time we got out the swinging double doors the small horde of zombies were getting too close for comfort. I stopped at the entry and accessed my orb of power, willing the zombies to stop their advance. Trying to affect that many undead was hard, to say the least. As it turned out, it was too hard. Zombies at the back of the room were still moving forward, even though I'd managed to stop the ones closest to us.

As I stood there concentrating with all of my might, I reached into a pouch on my vest and pulled out one of Smoke's handy thermite grenades. "Are you nuts?" Came Lori's incredulous voice behind me. "You'll bring this whole building down!"

"Hopefully not the whole building," I replied. "Everyone get the hell out now. I can't hold them back for long, and we can't let them get out of this building.

"What about you?" Said Lori urgently.

"I'm going to throw this grenade and run like hell," I said as I pulled the pin. The zombies were starting to overwhelm my powers. "Everybody run, now!" I shouted as I cocked my arm back for the throw.

The motion ended all arguments as everyone, but Petey turned and ran back down the hallway to the junction then headed out the main entrance. "Get going, Petey," I said through gritted teeth as my power began to crumble.

"I got your back boss," was all he said as he fended off a zombie that had managed to start moving our direction. "Damned brave, stupid noble idiot!" I thought as I threw the grenade towards the chemicals on the back wall.

"Run you idiot, now!" I shouted. I followed word with deed and turned to sprint down the hallway. Petey was right beside me. We made it about halfway down the main hall towards the entrance when the world heaved around us. A force like the fist of god slammed into our backs and sent us flying down the hall. That's the last thing I remembered before the world went black.

11

The jostling movement sent spikes of pain through my head. As my eyes cleared, I couldn't figure out why I was looking down at a pair of massive legs and combat boots moving across a dirty floor. I shook my head to try and clear it. That was a mistake as whoever was trying to drive the spikes through my skull, picked up a bigger hammer. A low moan escaped my lips.

"It's okay boss. I got ya." Came Petey's rumbling baritone.

Well, that explained the big legs and combat boots. "Put me down you big oaf," I said, starting to struggle weakly. The big arm wrapped around my legs just tightened a little further, immobilizing me quite efficiently.

"Just a sec boss. We're almost out." Croaked Petey through the smoke as it became lighter around us.

Suddenly there was shouting, and hands are grabbing at me. My head swam as I was laid on the sidewalk. As the scene came back into focus, I saw the team standing around looking concerned. Lori was crouched beside me, peeling an eyelid back to look at my pupils. I batted feebly at her hands. "I'm fine," I said grumpily, raising a hand towards Jake. "Help me stand up."

Jake looked over and got a nod from Lori before he offered a hand. Traitor. When I was once more vertical, I looked around and saw Petey leaning against one of the Suburbans. He was rumpled, and smoke stained but seemed to be okay.

I staggered over to him, as a marching band quick timed it through my cranium. "You okay?" I asked.

"I'm okay." He said nodding.

"Thanks for getting me out of there," I said, putting a hand on his shoulder. "Next time follow orders! I said angrily then, shoving him up against the vehicle.

Or rather I tried to shove him against the vehicle. The mountain of muscle didn't even move an inch. He just gave me a lopsided grin. "I got your back boss."

Knowing a lost cause when I saw one, I turned around to face the rest of the team. "Everybody else okay?" I asked as I scanned the faces and took in the billowing smoke emanating from the other side of the building.

"We're okay." Piped up Tommy. "On the other hand, You're an idiot."

There wasn't any heat in his words, however, so I just flipped him the bird and got back to business. "Let's clear out of here before the fire department arrives," I said turning once more to our vehicles. "Lori, get ahold of Alex and let him know what's going on," I said as I reached for a passenger door.

As we headed back towards headquarters, my phone started ringing. Fishing it out of my vest pocket I saw Siobhan's name on the screen. "What's up?" I said after hitting the accept button. "You're supposed to be asleep."

"Asleep? How can I sleep when I lose the sense of you, then get it back, only to lose it again!" Her voice grew ever louder as she worked her way to the end of the sentence.

"Yeah, sorry about…" That's all I managed to get out before she overrode me.

"Then, I get a call from my people telling me that the building you entered had just exploded! Do you know what that does to a girl's nerves?! She shouted "And then," She paused dramatically. "You don't even call to let me know you're okay. What the hell's up with that Dale?" She said as her tone went from one of anger down to that of a hurt little girl. My insides twisted in shame. No doubt just as she planned.

"I'm sorry," I said again, my head hanging a little. "You had to know I was alright, though." I finished lamely.

"You're not alright." She said softly then. "I know you're injured."

"It's just a bang to the head," I responded. "I didn't quite get out of the building in time."

A long-suffering kind of sigh sounded over the phone then. "Did you find your wife and daughter?" She asked.

"No," I said in resignation. "They weren't there. Neither was Ahriman. Just his shade again. Issuing orders."

"What kind of orders?" She asked suspiciously.

"The same one again." I sighed. "Give yourself up, or the wife and daughter face eternal torment. Yada yada yada. I said trying to play it off. It's hard to do that though when someone is tapped into the soul.

"You don't fool me, Dale," Siobhan said sternly. "You're contemplating something stupid." She said frankly.

I didn't bother to argue. "Look, just come over to headquarters when you can? We'll all sit down and make a plan."

"Very well." She said. "I will see you shortly." The phone clicked dead in my hand.

++++

"I'm thinking snipers," I said to the crowd sipping coffee in the ready room back at headquarters. It's the only way I can think of to convince Ahriman I'm alone and still have a backup.

My team, along with Siobhan and Alex, remained silent for a moment considering the idea. "Oakwood is huge boss," said Jake after a moment. It's going to be almost impossible to have someone in a good position to cover you, even if the whole team is spread out through the damned thing. Add to that, him having mojo of his own to detect us and he probably won't even show if we're there." Consternation was clearly visible on his face as he continued to consider our options.

"The size of Oakwood may be to our advantage in that regard," I responded. "How far out can this guy detect the living without actually seeing them?" I asked, turning to Siobhan.

She returned my gaze speculatively for a moment. "It is hard to tell. We don't know for sure what abilities he has." She was silent for a minute in thought. "Can you sense the living through your powers?" She asked abruptly.

"I...I don't know." I said as the thought struck me. It wasn't anything I'd tried before.

"Well, give it a whirl boss." Said Ray, waving around the room. "You've got a bunch of us right here.

I nodded my head nervously at him and lowered my head in concentration. It was tough to find my mojo with all those curious gazes on me, expecting me to pull miracles out of my ass.

Slowly the world outside my head faded to black, and I was able to access the mental image of my abilities. My orb of power. The tentacles of the undead emanated from it as usual, but for the life of me, I couldn't sense anything else. After a few more minutes of trying, I let out my breath in a gust and looked up at the room.

"Not a damned thing as far as living people go," I said, half in resignation, half in hope. It would have been a cool ability to have, but if I didn't, maybe Ahriman didn't either. I'm not a vampire or even undead, though." I said, looking at Siobhan. "What's your human being detection like?" I asked with a raised eyebrow.

"I detect humanity through my physical senses." Said Siobhan after a moment. "Horror movie cliches aside, I have hearing like a bat." She said with a sardonic twist of her mouth. "I can literally hear the blood rushing through your veins from twenty yards away if there isn't much background noise to filter out. And while I don't see any better than a human during the day, I have infravision at night that allows me to see human sized heat signatures from several hundred yards, with a clear line of sight."

"Okay," I said. We'll use that as our detection threshold." Siobhan had cleared her throat before I had a chance to continue. A total affectation on her part since she didn't need to breathe. "He may well have sorcerous methods of detection as well.

"Like what?" I asked.

"Wards of some kind come immediately to mind. As well as the field he placed around the building you blew up."

I considered what she said for a moment. "I can't imagine even Ahriman having the power to ward the entire perimeter of the cemetery. If anything he'll only be able to ward the entrances. As for the field he had cast over the building, I don't think that will be very useful unless he can't control the actions of any undead he's raised for the occasion."

"It also inhibits your ability to detect undead." Siobhan reminded me quickly.

"I don't think he's going to be trying to hide from me," I responded. "Like Jake pointed out earlier, Oakwood is a big place, and unless he's standing at one of the entrances, he's going to want me to track him down."

Over the next several hours we hammered out a plan, none of us were really happy about it, but it was the best we can come up with. I just hope it worked.

12

"This is my fight too, Dale! Every bit as much as it is yours!" Siobhan hissed.

The meeting broke up, and I'd sent everyone off to get some rest before the main event at midnight. What I'd hoped would be some energetic lovemaking followed by some much-needed sleep, devolved into an argument, almost immediately upon getting back to Siobhan's place.

I tried to remain calm and keep my voice level as she started in. "We've been over this," I said with a sigh. "We just don't know if your people will be able to withstand Ahriman's power. I said as gently as possible."

"You don't trust my ability to control my own?" Siobhan growled

"Of course I do!" I exclaimed. "What's more you know I do," I said reminding her of the link we shared.

"I cannot be seen to sit back and simply let humans handle our problems. It would be considered a weakness and there are several members of my family that would seek to use that to their own advantage." She growled

"This isn't about politics, Siobhan," I said, heat creeping into my own voice. "It's about waking up tomorrow!" I turned my back to her for a moment and took a couple of deep breaths.

"It's always about politics." She retorted hotly. "Perception is everything!"

"Bullshit!" I said, turning to face her once more. "All perception means is twisting the truth, so it looks like you want it to!" It was something I'd always hated about government and their lackeys in the media. And it irritated me to no end to hear it coming from my...girlfriend? Gulp.

"Don't be so naive, Dale. Siobhan's mouth twisted into a sneer. Manipulating facts to fit one's agenda has always been the way those in power control those beneath them." She said coldly.

"That doesn't make it right," I said as I turned back to face her, my eyes going cold.

"Right has very little to do with retaining power." She said, drawing herself up haughtily.

As I stood opposite her, I suddenly saw the master vampire that managed to control a major city. Gone was the loving girl, obsessed with my well being. In her place was a powerful creature of the night, who would not let anything stand in her way.

My shoulders slumped a little in sadness to see it. I knew it was there of course. Our link allowed for nothing less. The shock of seeing her front and center in this guise broke my heart a little. She had to have sensed my inner turmoil, but she stood firm in her convictions.

"You have to do what you think best Siobhan." I sighed. "But if one of your people comes after me or mine, we will defend ourselves," I said, letting her see the hunter at my core.

"I understand." She said, cooly

I turned and walked slowly to the door and opened it slowly. "I love you," I said quietly, not turning around and let the door shut behind me.

++++

I drove aimlessly for awhile in the golden afternoon light. The rumble of the Mustang and the speed metal of Metallica on the radio, helped me think.

Part of me felt the guilt of having someone new in my life. Especially since the corpses of my wife and daughter were still walking around. The hunter in me knew things would never be as they once were. It also knew that the best thing I could do for them now involved shotguns and big knives used for decapitation. Still, I wasn't sure it was something I could actually do. The doubt haunted me.

The hunter also had his doubts about Siobhan. How could there be any kind of personal relationship with quite possibly the most powerful undead entity that existed for hundreds of miles in any direction? She had shown me both sides of her nature. Which side would win out with me standing in the middle?

As the dark gray light of dusk settled over the city, I pulled into the parking structure of Nightstalker Inc. The lot was empty. No evidence that my team was anywhere around. I was supposed to go in alone after all.

Ahriman said I had to come alone. He didn't say anything about being unarmed when I showed up. I stood in front of my locker, looking at the instruments of death and defense that lived there for what seemed like a long time before I let out a sigh and started to suit up.

The pit in my stomach that I had since my argument with Siobhan slowly filled with lead as I put on my gear. Tactical pants and a black T-shirt were followed by a bulletproof vest, light amber shooting glasses and a kevlar helmet. Steel toed work boots rounded out the ensemble.

Next came the weapons. My Kimber 1911 went into his customary place on my hip, balanced by the familiar weight of the K-bar on the other side. As a little-added precaution, I slipped a small M&P .45. Into the thigh pocket of my tactical pants. It only held six shots, but as a last resort, it came in handy.

Shouldering my Saiga, I sighed and turned around to leave, catching sight of myself in a nearby mirror. I stood for a moment staring at the image of a stone cold operator in the mirror. I didn't feel near so tough on the inside.

Finally, I turned and headed out. As I walked, I sent out a thought towards Siobhan. She'd closed herself off to me after the argument. There was still a blank wall between us now. Sighing again, I trudged down the hall towards the elevator. Doing what needed to be done.

13

The big black Mustang slid through the night. Creedence Clearwater Revival sang to me about running through the jungle. It seemed appropriate somehow. Thirty minutes later, I rumbled to a stop outside the main entrance to Oakwood Cemetery. I cast my gaze around looking for a sign that I was being watched, but I couldn't see a damn thing but the large wrought iron fence and rows of grave markers that quickly faded into the darkness.

I approached the front gate and wasn't surprised at all when it opened with a jagged creaking sound beneath my touch. Opening it wide, I slipped in and closed it behind me. As I walked down the road leading from the gate, into the depths of the cemetery, I cast out my power trying to find where Ahriman was hiding.

The feel of undead started showing up to my power, winking on light spots of the night in my mind's eye. Some were brighter than others. Three, in particular, stood out to my attention. The brightest was Ahriman. It was so bright that it almost drowned at the lights nearby it. He couldn't hide them from me, however. The feeling of my wife and daughter even though horribly changed still beckoned to me like a siren's call.

Shaking my head, I tried to tune them out for a brief moment as I searched out and counted the other spots scattered around the cemetery. "Thirty besides Ahriman and my family," I said out loud to myself. "I thought he'd have more." Shrugging my shoulders I continued on in the darkness.

The road I was on, seemed to be leading me in more or less the right direction, so I felt no need to leave it for the time being. As I walked slowly down it, I could feel myself come to the attention of the undead around me. They were mostly zombies, with a ghoul or to thrown in for flavor. As I penetrated further towards my destination, the undead mass closed in and started following along behind me.

The smell of rot and freshly turned earth was the next thing my senses detected, followed quickly by the sound of moans and then the sight of the shuffling monsters, materializing out of the shadows. I paused, half raising the Saiga as one zombie, in particular, appeared from behind a headstone a short distance off the road beside me. He didn't attack, however. Instead, he just stood there slavering and moaning hungrily. More of them were coming up to me from behind, but again, none of them attacked. I finally figured it out. Ahriman had sent out a stinking, shuffling undead honor guard to escort me in. Lowering the Saiga I kept walking.

Before long the flickering light of ffire appeared through the trees. It wasn't very big, but I guessed that was my destination. The road curved gently in that direction, gradually bringing the fire into full view. The eerie orange light cast by a brazier balanced on three metal legs, cast flickering illumination on the figures behind it.

I stopped where I was. My eyes are greedily devouring the sight of my wife and, dear god, the form of Emily standing beside her. She was in a pale dress and looked up as my eyes fell on her, smiling adorably from behind soft curls of auburn hair. "Hi, Daddy." She said in her little girl voice. Momma said you'd come."

The statement caused my eyes to move on, taking in Samantha as she stood quietly between Emily and a robed figure. I couldn't see a face beneath the shadowed cowl of the robe, but I know it was Ahriman. Sam had an expression that was hopeful and fearful at the same time as she clutched at Emily's hand. The husband in me quailed to see that fear and longed to blast Ahriman out of existence.

The hunter in me just snorted derisively. "They look however Ahriman wants them to look." It said.

"You do not have the look of a man who has come as a willing sacrifice." Came Ahriman's voice from under the cowl.

"A guy's gotta be prepared in a neighborhood like this, late at night. Never know what's going to jump out at you." I said, gesturing at the undead around me.

"This is no time for flippancy, Mr. Frost." Growled Ahriman, throwing back the hood of his robe and glaring at me with his suddenly glowing green eyes. "Now," he said commandingly. "Drop your weapons and step forth."

His power washed over me as he made his demand, but it wasn't sufficient to crack the mental defenses that I'd worked diligently to put in place. His eyes widened briefly as he felt his power slide off my psyche. "Your vampire whore has taught you a few tricks, I see." He said, eyebrows drawing together in a scowl. "No matter." He continued. "You will submit to me willingly or not. The vampire will receive her chastisement in due course."

"Release my wife and daughter, and I'll submit. That's the deal." I said, putting steel in my voice. "Not before."

Ahriman chuckled at that. "You have no choice now, Mr. Frost." He said. "My children surround you. Walk forward and kneel or be dragged." He said gesturing at the zombies around me. "*Deals*, as you call them, are only valid if you can enforce them."

"You know, I figured you'd say something like that," I said with a growl as I reached into the thigh pocket of my pants and pulled out a thermite grenade. "So, I came prepared."

My left hand was coming up to pull the pin when a force hit me, taking me brutally to the ground in the blink of an eye. As I shook my head to clear my vision, the grenade was ripped brutally from my grip. "You can't hurt the Master daddy." Came my daughter's sweet voice from above me. Looking up, my heart crumbled in hurt and resignation as I saw her standing above me, holding the grenade and smiling sweetly around her fangs, her blood red eyes, dancing in delight.

"You humans are so predictable." Said Ahriman, from over by the brazier as dead hands grabbed me roughly and hauled me to my feet. "Always thinking you can save the day with your last second heroics."

Ahriman's zombie thugs started dragging me towards the brazier. Emily was back by Sam's side. They both seemed to be smiling in anticipation of what was to come. "So be it." I thought in resignation as the zombies pushed me down in front of it.

Looking for the things that used to be my wife and daughter, I looked over to meet Ahriman's gaze. "That wasn't the last second heroics," I said, gesturing to the sky with a single finger. "That was the distraction."

"What do you..." Started Ahriman as he was suddenly shoved to the side, pushing him out of the way of the silver cored, .50 caliber, high-velocity round. Unfortunately for the monster wearing the Samantha suit, the momentum of her movement to save her master brought her directly into the line of fire.

I stood frozen as titanic emotions warred with each other inside my soul. Anguish charged to the fore as I lost my wife once again. All the good times we had, flashed through my brain as grief tried to overwhelm me. Relief countered the charge, however, as I stared in horror at the grisly evidence that she would finally rest in peace.

Several things happened at once then. The heads of the zombies who'd been holding me exploded in viscous gore as they received their own high-velocity rounds. My reactions were automatic as my freed arms reached up to grab my Saiga.

"MOMMY!" Shouted Emily before blurring to her side, causing the .50 caliber round designated for her to miss. "Thank god! Dammit!" The father and the hunter inside me thought.

Emily stopped beside the growing pile of ash that had once been her mother. She stared down at it for a brief moment before looking back up and locking her eyes on mine. "You did this!" She hissed at me, blood red eyes glaring in hate. "You killed **Mommy!**" She shouted as she hurled the grenade she'd taken from me earlier, directly at me with speed and accuracy that no major league baseball pitcher on earth could hope to match.

Fortunately for me, little vampire girls don't typically know a lot about grenades, so she didn't pull the pin first. The one pound chunk of metal and chemicals collided solidly with my rising shotgun before ricocheting off and hitting me high in the chest. Even with the interference of the shotgun and the padding of my vest, the force still knocked me to the ground and caused the breath to woosh from my lungs.

As I lay there stunned amidst the legs of a mass of zombies, I felt Ahriman's power lash out in all directions. "Rise my children! Kill the intruders!" He shouted as he regained his feet.

The feel of his power and his shouted orders, got me going once more. As the zombies around me turned towards where the sound of the rifle fire had come from, I rose to my knees and brought the sights of my shotgun up to center squarely on Ahriman's head. Whatever else happened this night, Ahriman was going to die.

I stroked the trigger on the Saiga. Nothing happened. Looking down at the weapon in puzzlement, I saw that the impact of the grenade had crushed its upper receiver into a twisted mess. Cursing silently, I dropped it. As the shotgun swung on it's sling off to the side, I reached down to grab my .45 from the holster on my hip. My eyes are locked with Ahriman's in mutual hate as the big pistol rose in his direction. I was so focused on the act of putting the ancient necro down, that I didn't sense the attack until it was too late.

A weight crashed into me, hurling me to the ground once more and sent my .45 flying off into the night. Emily came up straddling my chest and began raining blows down on my head. I tried to fend them off with my arms, but she was too fast, too strong. I felt my nose break with a grinding crunch at the first blow. Pain exploded through my skull and tears filled my eyes, further inhibiting my ability to defend myself.

Blows continued to rain down; my vision narrowed down until I was looking through a dark, narrow tunnel. "Don't kill him child," Ahriman's voice came through the enshrouding darkness. "We need him alive for the sacrifice."

I heard a little girl growl as the slight weight of her body departed my torso. Small hands grabbed my arm roughly and started dragging me towards the brazier. Consciousness came and went in amongst waves of pain. The sounds of gunshots and shouting came to me during one moment of lucidity before pain engulfed me in darkness once more.

The next moment of lucidity came as I was thrown roughly on a long narrow stone bier, next to the flaming brazier. Emily's small form stood on the bier looking down at me with scorn and hate. Ahriman stood on the ground beside the long stone enclosure, looking at me with a similar expression. "Let me sacrifice him, master. Let me plunge the knife into his heart. She hissed around her fangs.

"Patience child." He said with an indulgent grin. "All things in due time. We must finish the ritual first."

The world continued to fade in and out. Moments of darkness interspersed with flashes of firelight. I tried feebly to resist as my arms and legs were roughly chained to the cold stone beneath me. All the resistance got me was another blow to the head from the monster that used to be my daughter. The world flashed white hot in pain briefly before going dark once more.

I was brought back to consciousness once more by the deep baritone sound of archaic words being intoned into the night. Ahriman stood at the head of the bier, hands spread wide in supplication as he recited the ritual that would end in my death. Firelight cast harsh shadows across his features as he spoke, giving a mad, evil cast to his features. I could feel his power gathering around us causing my skin to tingle as if I were hooked up to an electric charge.

On the bier next to me, stood Emily. She was dressed in a ceremonial robe of her own now. Orange and amber firelight reflected off of its shiny surface, making her seem to almost glow.
She held a large wicked looking dagger with both hands held high over her head, in preparation for plunging the jagged blade into my heart.

Ahriman's chant began raising in volume to a crescendo as I struggled in vain to free myself from the chains around my hands and feet .
"*Ereshkigal, nodanu I emuq a MITU!*" he shouted thunderously as his eyes met Emily's with a short nod.

Emily's blood red eyes flashed down to meet mine in savage glee as the dagger descended with blurring speed towards my chest. My hands strained against their bonds in an effort to block the lethal strike. A sound like someone hitting a side of beef with a sledgehammer cracked through the ai,r and Emily's coiled form was abruptly replaced by a crouched form in black leather with auburn hair flying wildly about her.

Siobhan was in her full vampire form. I got a brief glimpse of crimson eyes and two inch, needle sharp fangs set into the demonic visage of her inner beast. As abruptly as she appeared, she was gone. Another meaty impact was followed by a baritone shout of pain that sounded suspiciously like Siobhan trying to put her fist through Ahriman's chest.

The next instant she was back by my side, using her bare hands to break the shackles that held my wrists. "Took you long enough." I choked out as first one wrist; then the other were wrenched from of their restraints.

"I had to wait for him to be in the throws of his ritual before I acted." She said as she headed down to free my ankles. "Otherwise he'd have sensed my presence."

"My team? I muttered, sitting up as my right leg came free. Or short way off, I could see Emily's crumpled form amidst the rubble of a shattered headstone.

"They continue to fight on valiantly to reach you, but they are hard pressed. My people join in the fight even as we speak." She replied, heading towards the chains on my left ankle.

Her movement was halted suddenly, as an overwhelming power saturated the night. Ahriman stood tall once more. "You fool!" He said with utter contempt. "Did you think to beat me so easily?"

A vicious smile spread across his lips as Siobhan stared at him in horror, frozen in place...helpless. "I do have to thank you for the reinforcements, however, my dear." He said. "The minions I had summoned to repel this human's companions, seem to be unable to accomplish the task. It will be an easy thing to finish them off now that you have brought me so much help."

Siobhan moaned and dropped to her knees as I felt Ahriman's power ratchet up once more. Instinctively I reached out to connect with her once more.

The pressure being put on Siobhan's formidable defenses was crushing. It was taking everything she had, simply to keep him at bay. Even at that, her shield was slowly deforming under the onslaught. I pushed all the power I had through our bond, and Siobhan began to fight back.

Ahriman's features drew down in consternation as Siobhan began to push back. Her mental shield firmed back up, and she stood up from her kneeling position, hands raised towards him as if she could physically push back his power.

I could feel the blanket of power that Ahriman cast around the cemetery begin to falter and recede back toward him as he was forced to focus more and more power into the fight with Siobhan. Leaning forward, I reached into my thigh pocket and pulled out the little MP5 pistol, raising it to put the sights on Ahriman's chest. I was way to shaky to try a head shot.

My finger started to squeeze the trigger when a hiss sounded from the darkness. Emily's leaping form came into the firelight. Her hands were stretched out in front of her, forming themselves into claws. Her mouth was distended unnaturally giving free reign to her fangs to bite and rend. The smudged and torn robe she wore, nevertheless glowed amber in the firelight as she flew towards me.

I saw all this in an instant as my sights centered on her and the pistol bucked in my hand with two sharp explosions. My aim was good enough; both shots took her in the chest. One silver bullet transfixed her heart. The pain I felt in my own heart as her limp body crashed at the foot of the bier, felt even worse.

I couldn't let myself dwell on it, however, as the battle between Siobhan and Ahriman continued. Ahriman had the advantage once more as the attack by Emily had broken my concentration. I tried in vain to push power at Siobhan, but I had nothing left. The night of pain and the constant battle had tapped my reserves.

There was only one thing left to do. I raised the .45 in my hand and put my last four bullets into Ahriman's chest. He staggered back as the bullets impacted his sternum and ribcage, coming to rest against a headstone. Then he stood back up, smiling. "I admire your tenacity, human but I am beyond death. I am beyo..." His words were cut off, literally, as the silvered blade of a battle axe whistled through the night and impacted with brutal strength against Ahriman's neck. The head tumbled into the night as the rest of the body crumbled to dust.

I stared in shock for a moment. Part of me kept expecting Ahriman to coalesce before me and resume the fight. Instead, an immense form stepped through the swirling dust of Ahriman's remains. He was battered and bloody. He had a limp that said he was going to need some medical attention and his brutish face may have been the most beautiful thing I'd ever seen.

Petey looked at me and slowly winked. "I got your back boss." He said with a smile.

I hopped off the bier to go check on people. Or at least I tried to. In all the action, I'd forgotten that I still had one leg chained to the damned thing. The resulting demonstration in the laws of physics left me sprawled on by back beside the bier, one leg hanging awkwardly above me.

"Smooth," said a female voice above me and I looked up to see Siobhan smiling down at me sardonically.

"A little help here?" I asked plaintively, gesturing up at my ankle.

Siobhan's grin remained as she walked over and casually used her superhuman strength to pry open the shackle. The smile faltered and turned to an expression of profound sadness as she took in the sight of Emily's crumpled form lying at the foot of the bier. "Oh Dale, I..I'm so sorry," she said as a trembling hand came to her lips.

I stood up slowly, staring at my daughter as her body came into view behind the huge chunk of granite. Shooting the heart of a vampire with a silver bullet can stop them for awhile, but it doesn't kill them. For that, you had to take the head.

Standing to my full height, I held out my hand to Petey as he came up beside me. "No boss." He said reluctantly. "Let me take care of her. No father should have to do this."

"Let him handle it," Siobhan said softly. "This is too much for anyone."

"I can't," I said through trembling lips as I tried to keep my composure. "I have to do it myself," I said in a hoarse whisper.

"But, why?" Petey asked innocently as a tear ran down his boyish face.

"Because I couldn't forgive the person who did it," I said as the hand I continued to hold out to Petey started to tremble.

Our gazes are locked in a moment of understanding and Petey slowly handed me his axe. Siobhan stepped out of the way. Blood red tears leaked from the corner of her eyes. As I moved to Emily's side, the rest of the Dreadnoughts slipped silently out of the darkness to stand silently beside me. They were battered and bleeding, every one of them. Lori wept openly, her sniper rifle hanging limply from her shoulder.

In her unconscious state, Emily's features had returned to that of an innocent little girl. I studied her face hard, etching into my memory for eternity, her angelic face. It was all I had left.

The axe rose and fell burying itself deeply into the ground as my little angel turned to dust.

Epilogue

Thanks, in large part, to Siobhan and her people, my Dreadnoughts and I had survived. The Dreadnoughts had been cornered against the fence that surrounded the cemetery. Running low on ammo, they'd hunkered down behind the shield wall, and used blades and the occasional well-aimed pistol shot, to keep the horde at bay. That's where Siobhan's people found them. Zombies are no match against vampires. The bite that turns humans into zombies has no effect at all against those who are already dead.

The vampires dared not get any closer to Ahriman than they had already, however. They felt his compulsion even at the edge of his range. A couple of the younger vamps had to be restrained by their elders so that they didn't start attacking the Dreadnoughts themselves.

That left it up to my boys and girls to come to the rescue. They'd spread out to come at it from all angles and either by God's will or blind luck; Petey got there in time.

It was Siobhan herself that kept me going after the axe fell. Through our bond, she managed to keep the pieces of my shattered soul together as I rocked back and forth silently in her arms. It's in too many pieces to ever go back to what it was before, but with her help, at least it'll have a chance to heal, a little anyway. It doesn't really feel like it right now, though. I don't want to talk about it.

As we trudged slowly back to the entrance of the cemetery, Lori came up beside me. She was still crying. "Dale," she choked out. "I'm s...sorry." Her shoulders started to shake as sobs started wracking her body.

I stopped where I was and enfolded her in a tight embrace. "You have nothing to apologize for," I said in puzzlement. "What's wrong?"

"I missed the shot." She sobbed into my chest. "O...On Emily. Because of me, you had to...end it yourself.

I tightened my grip and stroked her hair, trying to ease the pain. You're the only person on earth I could allow to take those shots other than myself, and you saved me from having both of their existences on my conscious. You did good, Lori. I wouldn't be alive without you."

We stayed that way for a couple more moments before Lori disengaged and wiped her nose. "Thanks, boss," she said with a watery smile, and we turned to catch up with the group.

Alex was waiting by the entrance for us with a look of profound relief on his face as he saw that everyone who went in, came out. He walked over to me with an outstretched hand. "Is it...over?" He asked anxiously.

I nodded but was unable to talk suddenly. He looked into my eyes. I'm not sure what he saw, but his other hand came up to squeeze my shoulder briefly before stepping back. "We'll go clean up the mess," he said, after clearing his throat self-consciously. "Go get some sleep or something."

"Thanks," I said, turning to face my Dreadnoughts. "Drinks are on me, boys and girls," I said as I put my arm around Siobhan's shoulders. "We have a lot of celebrating and mourning to do." I finished with a catch in my throat. That's the life of we few who stalk the night.

++++

A shadow, lost amongst shadows, slipped silently between headstones, hiding from the light of the flashlights that played over the scene of his defeat. The local authorities were cleaning up the mess. Here and there the corpses of his children could be seen in the harsh light. Seen, that is if Ahriman still had eyes. That ability, along with all his other abilities had been robbed from him once more.

He still existed, however. No mere weapon of man could take that away from him. Long ago, he'd mastered the abilities of the Lich. So long as his soul stayed safely in its hidden reliquary, he would continue to exist and plot his revenge.

The end

Thank you for reading!

Like what you read? Questions? Comments? Let me know.

https://www.facebook.com/Art-DeForest-17030446 89948412/

http://www.amazon.com/-/e/B01CDKZA0O

I like to talk with everybody and I'll do my best to talk to you.

Art DeForest

Books by Art DeForest

Kaitlyn Strong

Hunter's Saga

Printed in Great Britain
by Amazon